RUDE AWAKENING

Rosalind had sailed from America afloat on a dream of love. But on England's shore, she was brought sharply down to earth.

Why was Lord Philip Southvale not there to embrace her as his bride, but instead remain mysteriously missing?

Why did the splendid portrait of his exquisitely beautiful first wife still dominate his study?

Why was that woman's overbearingly arrogant brother, Gerald Beaufort, there to greet Rosalind with a mixture of pity and scorn that left her trembling with rage?

So many questions . . . with answers that threatened to turn hope into heartbreak . . .

As the daughter of an officer in the Royal Air Force, Sandra Heath spent most of her life traveling around to various European posts. She has lived and worked in both Holland and Germany. The author now resides in Gloucester, England, together with her husband and young daughter, where all her spare time is spent writing. She is especially fond of exotic felines, and at one time or another, has owned each breed of cat.

ROMANTIC ENCOUNTERS

The Second Lady Southvale

by

Sandra Heath

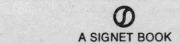

A SIGNET BOOK

NEW AMERICAN LIBRARY

A DIVISION OF PENGUIN BOOKS USA INC.

NAL BOOKS ARE AVAILABLE AT QUANITY DISCOUNTS WHEN USED TO
PROMOTE PRODUCTS OR SERVICES. FOR INFORMATION PLEASE WRITE
TO PREMIUM MARKETING DIVISION, NEW AMERICAN LIBRARY,
1633 BROADWAY, NEW YORK, NEW YORK 10019.

SIGNET TRADEMARK REG. U.S.PAT. OFF. AND FORIEGN COUNTRIES
REGISTERED TRADEMARK—MARCA REGISTRADA
HECHO EN DRESDEN, TN., U.S.A.

SIGNET, SIGNET CLASSIC, MENTOR,ONYX, PLUME, MERIDIAN and
NAL BOOKS are published by New American Library, a division of Penguin
Books USA Inc., 1633 Broadway, New York, New York 10019

First Printing, March, 1990

1 2 3 4 5 6 7 8 9

PRINTED IN THE UNITED STATES OF AMERICA

1

If there was one thing that was certain to cause a stir at the Fourth of July ball at the Carberry mansion in Washington, especially in 1811, when America and Britain were again moving toward war, it was the entirely inappropriate arrival of an English lord who appeared to be the embodiment of all his nation's old-world arrogance.

The ball had been proceeding very agreeably until the announcement of Lord Southvale's name, and Washington society had been enjoying to the full the lavish hospitality of the great house on the southern outskirts of the capital. Mr. William Carberry was a wealthy and influential man, and his wife was one of the city's finest hostesses, which meant that invitations to their residence were much sought after, and very few persons of consequence were absent. Lights blazed in every room, hundreds of lanterns glowed in the gardens, and the sound of music drifted out into the humid summer night, where countless insects throbbed unseen in the surrounding darkness. There were few thoughts of impending war as everyone turned their attention to the pursuit of pleasure.

One face was glaringly absent from the occasion, however, for the Carberry's son and heir, John, had failed to put in an appearance. Not that anyone was really surprised, for his conduct over the past year had left a great deal to be desired. Before then he'd been a model son, and a credit to his parents, but now he was more often in drink than not, and was usually to be found losing heavily at the gaming tables. The change stemmed from a fateful afternoon the previous July, when his reckless driving of a curricle had caused the death of his beloved fiancée, Elizabeth Mackintosh. Now he was plagued with grief and guilt, and took refuge in the bottle; but if cognac dulled the pain for a while, it also unleashed the sort of irresponsible behavior that a strict disciplinarian like his father found impossible to condone. In Mr. William Carberry's view, a year was more than sufficient time to adjust to bereavement, and a vast improvement in conduct was now expected. Sadly, it was an improvement that had yet to show any sign of coming into being.

William Carberry and his wife had a second child, however, a daughter named Rosalind, and not only was she present at the ball, she was also the credit to her parents that her wayward brother had ceased to be. She was twenty-two years old, a little above medium height, and gracefully slender, with a glory of long golden curls that tonight were worn in a very becoming Grecian style. Her skin was pale and clear, and her large green eyes were unexpectedly dark-lashed, so that they were very arresting and memorable indeed. She liked to wear green, because it brought out the color of her eyes, and tonight she wore a high-waisted, décolleté gown made of sheer ice-green silk, with glass-bead decoration on the bodice, little sleeves, and hem. Long white gloves encased her arms, a knotted white shawl trailed on the floor behind her, and there was an ivory fan looped over her wrist. Her only jewelry was a pair of exquisite drop emerald earrings that had been left to her by her grandmother.

A polonaise was in progress, and she was dancing with George Whitby, the young man she was widely expected to soon accept in marriage. He was a little older than she, and good-naturedly attractive in a sandy-haired, rather freckled way. He'd been paying court to her for six months now, and while neither of their hearts had been truly engaged, they were nevertheless fond enough of each other for her to be seriously considering him as her future husband. Her parents' marriage hadn't been a love match, but had been arranged for them, and their subsequent happiness was sufficient inducement for her to believe a similar match would be right for her.

She was enjoying the evening, until a glance at the gilded clock on the wall above the orchestra's gallery reminded her that it was nearly midnight, and John was still nowhere to be seen. She sighed, for he was a constant source of worry to her. She knew how deeply he'd loved Elizabeth, and knew too that he'd always blame himself for her death, but he was destroying himself because of it, and his sister could only stand helplessly by, for he wasn't open to reason. She'd thought he'd paid a little attention to her that morning, however, when he'd promised to attend the ball in order to smooth over his many recent differences with his father, but evidently it was a promise already forgotten.

The polonaise continued, and George smiled at her as they danced. Rosalind returned the smile, determined not to let her anxiety over John spoil her own enjoyment of the occasion, but at that very moment an announcement was made that proved that John had remembered his promise after all. Two very late arrivals had appeared at the top of the ballroom steps, and as the master of ceremonies struck the floor with his staff, Rosalind turned to see her brother and a tall, dark, exceedingly handsome gentleman whose name was given as Philip de Grey, Lord Southvale.

The ball came to a startled and abrupt halt, and a ripple of whispers spread throughout the distinguished gathering. Rosalind stared at her brother in dismay, noting the slight flush on his cheeks that once again told of a little too much cognac. He was the worse for wear, as he surely had to be to have brought a British nobleman like Lord Southvale to a Fourth of July ball!

Her glance moved to the lord in question. She knew a little about him, for word had traveled when he'd arrived in the capital a few days earlier in the entourage of the new British envoy, Mr. Augustus Foster, who'd been dispatched by London in a last attempt to avert war. Mr. Foster was known to be tactfully remaining in the legation on this of all nights, but Lord Southvale was evidently of a very different and much more provocative stamp.

She studied the Englishman in those brief startled seconds. He was in his late twenties, she guessed, and almost too handsome. His thick, wavy hair was the color of coal, and the eyes with which he coolly surveyed the ballroom were a vivid, piercing blue. There was something arrogantly and lazily British about him, for he was every inch the aristocratic London Carinthian, and yet there was a nonchalance in his manner that suggested indifference to the stir his arrival had caused. A starched neckcloth burgeoned discreetly at this throat, his black velvet coat was deliberately cut too tight to be buttoned, and his white satin waistcoat was set off to perfection by the spill of rich lace adorning the front of his shirt. His hips and legs were encased in white silk breeches that managed to reveal every outline of his manly shape, and the shine on his black leather pumps showed that his valet took his duties very seriously indeed.

As the astonished guests continued to whisper, George moved a little closer to Rosalind. "John appears to have excelled himself this time," he murmured.

"I fear so," she replied, glancing quickly toward her parents. Her father, tall, distinguished, and graying, looked positively thunderous, and her mother, a rounded, still-pretty woman in peach satin, looked a little faint.

"The grieving widower grieves no more, it seems," said George, his disapproving gaze fixed upon Lord Southvale.

"I beg your pardon?"

"Surely you've heard the tale of the late Lady Southvale?" Philip de Gray's beautiful and adored young wife, the former Miss Celia Beaufort, had been lost in a shipwreck off the coast of Ireland the previous year, while on her way to visit her family, and her body had never been recovered. There were distant Beaufort cousins in Washington, and so the story had circulated American drawing rooms as well as British.

"Yes, of course I know the tale," Rosalind replied, "but why do you speak so disparagingly of him as a grieving widower who grieves no more?"

"Because I was told that he hadn't attended a single social occasion since his wife's death, and because when I was introduced to him yesterday, I noticed that he was still wearing his wedding ring. He isn't wearing it now."

Rosalind's gaze moved to Lord Southvale's left hand, so clearly visible as he toyed with the lace at his cuff. Unlike most of the gentlemen present, he wasn't wearing white gloves, and it was true; there wasn't a wedding ring on his finger.

George touched her arm suddenly. "Your mother is endeavoring to catch your eye," he said.

She turned quickly, and her mother gestured toward the two new arrivals. Rosalind's heart sank, for it was plain her mother wished her to greet them and thus attempt to take a little of the sting out of the situation.

George's hand rested reassuringly beneath her elbow. "I think she's right. She can't go herself, for by the look of your father, he's about to declare war prematurely."

"Will you come with me?"

"If you wish."

Her pulse quickened as she and George began to make their way across the floor toward the foot of the ballroom steps. Their progress was closely observed, and fans and quizzing glasses were raised as fresh whispers broke out.

John had perceived his sister's approach and began to lead his guest down to meet her. Rosalind fixed her brother with a dark look, for his smile was a little lopsided and his steps very slightly unsteady. He was two years her senior, with the same blond hair and green eyes, and even when in drink he was possessed of an infectious and irrepressible charm.

He wore an embroidered mulberry velvet coat and cream silk breeches, and he grinned at her as he sketched a rather lavish bow.

"Ah, sweet Rosie, how delectable you look tonight, but then you always do." He nodded at George. "Good evening, George."

"John."

Rosalind was looking furiously at her brother. "Don't call me Rosie, you know I hate it!" Then she remembered that her mother wished her to defuse the situation, not add to it, and she made herself smile in an outwardly agreeable way, but her green eyes flashed to show him that he'd incurred more than her mild displeasure.

The orchestra suddenly struck up a lively country dance, and from the corner of her eye she saw her parents taking to the floor in an endeavor to get the ball into swing again. The other guests hesitated, but then several couples began to dance as well, and before long everything was proceeding again, but not in quite the same mood as before, for too much attention was still upon the small party at the foot of the steps.

John still seemed unaware of his faux pas. "Sis, may I present my good friend Philip de Grey, Lord Southvale? Philip, this is my sister, Rosalind, and this is a close family friend, Mr. George Whitby."

Lord Southvale didn't look at her at first, but bowed to George. "Your servant, sir."

George politely returned the salute, but with a rather wry smile. "My servant? I doubt that very much, sir."

The Englishman's sharp blue eyes flickered over him, but not icily, for there was a hint of humor in their glance. Then he turned to her. "I'm honored to make your acquaintance, Miss Carberry," he said softly, raising her gloved hand to his lips.

His voice was low and vibrant, and now that she was really close, she thought him even more handsome than she had before. His face was romantically good-looking, fine-boned but not in any way weak, and his lips curved in a way that told her he would be quick to smile. She was suddenly very unsettled, for his gaze was disconcertingly direct, and even though he'd kissed her gloved hand, she felt as if his lips had brushed her naked skin.

The many glances from the guests at last made an impression on John. He ran his fingers through his blond hair and smiled a little sheepishly at George. "I've put my foot in it again, haven't I?"

"Just a little."

Lord Southvale was apologetic. "The fault is mine, I fear. I'd have been wiser to have stayed away."

Rosalind was in crushing agreement. "You would indeed, sir."

John was appalled with her. "Sis, have you no manners?"

She wasn't repentant. "Well, it's true, he *would* have been wiser." Her green eyes rested critically upon the Englishman. "If you're here on a diplomatic mission intended to avert war, sir, diplomacy would appear to be the very quality in which you're somewhat lacking."

He smiled a little. "You're quite right to be angry with me, Miss Carberry, for I fully deserve it, but I am anxious to repair any damage my tactlessness may have caused. It's too late to undo what's already been done, and if I were to leave again immediately, it would look even more glaring, so perhaps we should just observe dull convention for a while, before I discreetly remove my unlovely British hide from this place."

She wasn't sure of him, for his reaction to her attack wasn't what she'd expected. "Observe dull convention?" she repeated cautiously. "What, exactly, does that mean?"

He glanced toward the dance floor, where the country dance would soon end. "I believe it would be appropriate if you honored me with the next dance, Miss Carberry. War may be in the air, but it hasn't quite broken out yet, and neither of us will be guilty of high treason if we tread a measure together.'' He smiled at her, his eyes warm and just a little teasing. There was no suggestion of cool mockery in his glance, just a wish to put matters right.

She hesitated.

He smiled again. ''At least allow me the chance to right the wrong, Miss Carberry.''

She met his eyes and found herself returning the smile. ''Very well, sir,'' she said.

The country dance finished, and a minuet was announced. He took her hand, leading her onto the dance floor. His fingers were warm and firm around hers, and again she felt as if he touched her bare skin. She was acutely conscious of everything about him, and her heart had begun to beat unaccountably more swiftly. A breathless sense of anticipation enveloped her, an excitement that had stirred instantly into life when he'd smiled into her eyes. This man, this English lord, was different from all the men she'd met before, compellingly different . . .

2

There was something dreamlike about that minuet. She barely heard the orchestra, and yet her steps didn't falter as she was led effortlessly through the precise sequence of steps.

Faces she knew swam past. She saw her mother still endeavoring to divert her father, whose controlled anger was directed not at Lord Southvale, but at John. John was still with George, and looked a good deal more sober now as he contemplated the likely parental reaction to this latest example of his excesses. George watched Rosalind as she danced, and his face was thoughtful. Other eyes were upon her, too, as the cream of Washington society observed the telltale flush on her cheeks as she danced with the handsome English lord.

As the minuet at last came to an end, Rosalind and Lord Southvale found themselves close to the French windows that stood open onto the lantern-lit terrace. The orchestra played the final notes, and she sank into a curtsy.

He held her hand for a moment longer than required. "Miss Carberry, a breath of fresh air would be more than agreeable to me. Would you care to accompany me onto the terrace?" He spoke softly, his voice barely audible as a ländler was announced and couples began to take up their positions.

She had to reluctantly shake her head. "My father wouldn't approve, Lord Southvale."

"Such a brightly lit terrace is hardly a den of impropriety, Miss Carberry. Besides, I see quite a number of guests out there, so good conduct will be seen to be observed." He smiled into her green eyes.

Her halfhearted resistance crumbled away. "You're quite right, sir, so I would be pleased to accompany you." She was conscious of a frisson of pleasure as he took her hand again, drawing it over his arm.

She heard whispering break out again behind them as they stepped out of the ballroom, but she didn't glance back. The guests who were already on the terrace made little secret of observing the evening's most fascinating twosome, and the color heightened on Rosalind's cheeks, but Lord Southvale gave no sign of being aware of the stir they were causing.

He led her to the stone balustrade at the edge of the terrace and then stood looking at the lights of Washington twinkling to the north across a moonlit expanse of alder-studded marshland. The music coming from the ballroom behind them competed with the throb of insects, and from time to time fireworks exploded in the sky above the capital as America celebrated its independence from British rule.

A large formal rose garden stretched away from the foot of the terrace, filling the night with perfume. Lanterns illuminated the paths and lit up the magnificent blooms that were Rosalind's mother's pride and joy. At the far end, against a white picket fence and a windbreak of tall evergreens, stood a little summerhouse where it was good to sit at this time of the year. To the south, away from Washington, the silver ribbon of the Anacostia River swept toward its confluence with the Potomac, and in the distance all around, palely lit by the moon, was the hilly, wooded countryside where Rosalind liked to ride. George often accompanied her on her rides, and as she stood by Lord Southvale in the lantern light, she felt a pang of conscience. In all the time she'd known George, she's never experienced anything that came even remotely close to the tumbling, bewildering emotions that had seized her during these past few minutes.

Her gloved hands trembled a little as she rested them on the stone balustrade. She felt she had to say something. Anything. "It—it must be a little dull for you to be here instead of enjoying the London Season."

"Not really. I happen to find Washington very much to my liking."

"But surely it's a little rustic here after the sophistication of London?"

"Rustic?" He smiled, glancing up at the mansion rising against the sky behind them. "I'd hardly call this rustic, Miss Carberry."

His smiles played havoc with her already unsettled composure, and she strove to appear quite calm and unconcerned as she continued the conversation. "Maybe this particular house is grand enough, sir, but Washington as a whole is somewhat unfinished, you have to admit. The houses are scattered, the public buildings incomplete, and the roads and sidewalks tend to peter out here and there. And listen to the insects. We're in the middle of a virtual swamp."

"I cannot argue with what you say, but I can see what Washington will be like in the future, and I like what I see."

He gazed toward the city, and as he did so, his right hand moved slightly on the balustrade. A flash of gold on his finger caught her eye. Had he transferred his wedding ring from his other hand? No, it wasn't a wedding ring, it was a signet ring. By the light of the lanterns she could make out the design that was cut into the ring; it was a griffin, the mythical beast that was the emblem of the de Grey family.

He glanced at her again. "As to the second part of your question . . ."

"My question?"

"Whether or not I miss the London Season. I have to confess that socializing hasn't been very much to my taste this past year; indeed, this is the first time I've indulged in such diversions since my wife died."

She felt dreadful. "Oh, forgive me, I didn't mean to—"

"I know you didn't, Miss Carberry, and I promise that I haven't taken offense." His eyes were very blue as he studied her. "Can you similarly promise me that you haven't taken offense because of my intrusion here tonight?"

"Yes, Lord Southvale, I can promise you that." It was true, for although he'd angered her at first, that was most certainly no longer the case.

"I'm relieved to hear you say so, for the last thing I wished to do was tread upon any sensitive toes."

She was curious. "Why *did* you come? This is a Fouth of July ball, Britain isn't exactly popular here at the moment, and quite a number of my parents' guests happen to believe that war is the only way to settle the differences between our two countries. Your envoy, Mr. Foster, has prudently stayed at the legation tonight, but you've taken it upon yourself to come here. Why?"

"For a very selfish and personal reason, if the truth be known," he murmured.

"I can't even begin to imagine what such a reason might be, sir."

"No, I'm sure you can't." He smiled at her. "Has anyone ever told you that you're a remarkably beautiful and engaging young lady?" he asked suddenly.

The apparent change of tack caught her off-guard. "I—I beg your pardon?"

"Come now, surely the American male hasn't been so remiss as to neglect to pay you the compliments you're due?"

Color rushed into her cheeks again. "You flatter me, I think," she replied in embarrassment, thoroughly disconcerted by her continuing susceptibility to everything about him.

"No, Miss Carberry," he said softly, "I'm not flattering you at all. I'm being very direct and honest. *You* are the reason I've come here tonight."

She stared at him.

He held her gaze. "This morning I happened to look out

of the legation in Seven Buildings, and saw an open landau drive from Nineteenth Street into Pennsylvania Avenue. There was a young lady seated inside, wearing a lime-green muslin pelisse and matching gown. She had golden hair and she twirled a frilled white parasol above her head. I thought her the most delightful creature I'd ever seen, and I made it my business to find out who she was. The Carberrys are very well-known in Washington, and it didn't take long to learn your name."

She didn't know what to say. Her cheeks felt as if they were on fire, and her pulse had quickened almost unbearably. She looked quickly around the terrace and saw that many glances were still being directed surreptitiously toward her and her noteworthy companion.

He smiled a little. "If I'm embarrassing you, you must forgive me, Miss Carberry, but you did ask me why I came here tonight." His blue eyes moved slowly over her flushed face. "By pure chance I was told that your brother was to be found at a certain gaming house, and so I took myself there in order to make his acquaintance."

"Does—does John know why you wished to come here tonight?"

"No. He invited me because it's his belief war is only encouraged if the protagonists refuse to associate."

She looked away. "I'll warrant the cognac had something to do with it."

"Possibly. Whatever his reason, I didn't argue, but took him up immediately on his invitation. The rest you know."

For a long moment she was silent, but then she looked at him again. "Are you always this direct, Lord Southvale?"

"It isn't something I make a habit of, Miss Carberry," he said softly, "but I tell you this, I've never before so desired an introduction that I'd resort to any means to acquire it. I saw you, and I had to know you, it's as simple as that."

She stared at him, her heart pounding wildly in her breast. None of this was really happening, it couldn't be happening . . . But it was happening, and spellbinding emotions were arousing thoughts and feelings she'd never known before.

His hand moved to briefly touch hers. "Have you nothing to say?"

"I don't know what to say," she whispered, a shiver of pleasure trembling through her just at the fleeting contact.

"Haven't you felt anything since our meeting?" he asked. "Are you immune to me?"

"No woman could ever be immune to you, Lord Southvale."

A faint smile played on his lips. "I'm not concerned about other women, just about you. Look at me."

Slowly she obeyed, and was conscious of a powerful current that seemed to almost leap between their eyes.

"Are you going to marry George Whitby?" he asked quietly, holding her gaze.

"I don't know . . ." Nothing was certain anymore. What had been clear at the commencement of the evening was all in question now. How could she marry George now that she'd experienced such soaring emotion from just being with this Englishman? The feelings she'd had for George were as nothing when set beside the shivering delight of merely receiving one of Philip de Grey's devastating smiles.

"Has he asked you to marry him?" he pressed.

"Yes."

"But you haven't accepted?"

"No."

His hand moved over hers again, but not fleetingly this time. The caress destroyed her resistance, and her gloved fingers involuntarily curled to meet his. She felt the hardness of his signet ring as he held her hand tightly, but then she remembered everyone else on the terrace and hurriedly drew away.

"No, we mustn't . . ."

"It's too late now, Rosalind, for I've seen into your heart," he said softly.

She swallowed, her tongue passing nervously over her

lower lip. "But we hardly know each other, Lord Southvale."

"I know all I need to about you."

"But I know very little about you."

"That's easily corrected. Meet me tomorrow."

"I can't do that," she gasped. This was all happening far too quickly, and she felt as if all control was being taken from her.

"Why not?" His tone was softly persuasive and his eyes teased her to defy her heart.

"Why not? Because it isn't done for a lady to make assignations with a gentleman she's only just been introduced to."

"Nor is it done for said lady to clasp said gentleman's hand so intimately, or to let him see in her eyes that she desires him as much as he desires her."

Her breath caught, and confusion beset her. "Please, stop . . ." she whispered.

"Stop? And see the prize slip from my fingers? No, Rosalind, I don't intend to let that happen. I want you more than anything else in this world, and time isn't on my side if I wish to win you."

"Time?" She could barely collect her scattered thoughts. She could hear his voice, but her own heartbeats threatened to drown his words.

"I may not be in Washington for very long. My task here is to be the messenger boy, should there be any significant developments in the talks between the British envoy and the American government. I'm due to go to St. Petersburg at the beginning of next year, and was only sent here at the last minute because the diplomat who was to have come was hurt in a riding accident. If I'm sent back to London because of the talks, someone else will return to Washington in my place, and I am still going to Russia in the new year. It's because time may be very short that I've pressed you so tonight, for if I'd allowed convention to take its course, I could have found myself on my way home to London without progressing beyond a formal introduction.'' Shaking his head a little, he gave a short, rather incredulous laugh. "Dear God, I'd never have dreamed it possible to have been so struck by lightning that I'd behave like this.''

"That's how I feel too,'' she said quietly, for it was true.

"Then you know we have to meet again?''

"Yes.'' What point was there in pretending otherwise? She wanted to see him, to be with him . . .

"Tomorrow?''

She nodded.

"Or should I say today, for I believe it's now the Fifth of July.''

She smiled. "Yes, it is.''

"John told me that you and he often ride in the woods east of here.''

"Yes, we do.''

"He mentioned a fallen tree on a hill, from where there's a particularly spectacular view.''

"Yes.''

"I'll be there at midday.''

"I'll come to you,'' she whispered.

"And now I think perhaps it's time I left, don't you?''

She glanced around the terrace and saw that interest in them hadn't diminished. "Maybe it would be best,'' she agreed reluctantly, for she didn't want him to go.

"Would you apologize to your parents on my behalf? I really didn't intend to cause such a stir.''

"I'll tell them.''

He looked deep into her eyes. "Good night, Rosalind,'' he said softly.

"Good night, Philip.'' It seemed the most natural thing in the world to call him by his first name, because suddenly he was everything in the world to her.

He left, walking quickly away across the terrace and into the ballroom. The inevitable whispers accompanied his every step, but he gave no indication of noticing anything. As he made his exit from the ballroom a minute or so later, a positive babble of conversation broke out, and Mrs. Carberry again felt compelled to order the orchestra to play a lively dance.

Rosalind remained on the terrace, gazing out over the rose garden. More fireworks exploded in the night sky above the capital, bursting in colorful brilliance in the darkness.

She felt rather than heard George's light step behind her, then he was by her shoulder. "Rosalind, I trust you know what you may be getting yourself into," he said quietly.

"I don't understand . . ." she began, intending to feign innocence, but then he put his hand gently to her elbow.

"Don't pretend with me, for there isn't any need."

She looked quickly away.

He smiled. "We've never been in love with each other, Rosalind, but we're close enough for me to know that something very important has happened to you tonight. I'm man enough to take my disappointment on the chin, and I'm friend enough to want to warn you to take care. There are many obstacles between you and a man like Philip de Grey, and not the least of those obstacles is his love for his wife."

She stared at him.

"He wore his wedding ring only yesterday, Rosalind. Just remember that." He hesitated, and then kissed her cheek gently before turning and walking away.

3

Very little was said at the Carberry breakfast table the following morning. Rosalind's father was in a dark mood as he read his newspaper, and her mother was on edge, waiting for the mood to spill over into an angry confrontation with John. No one mentioned the ball, and the laughter and conversation that usually followed the Fourth of July was noticeably absent.

John was suffering the aftereffects of his overindulgence in cognac, and his face was gray as he poured himself his third cup of black coffee. His blond hair was tousled and his green eyes lackluster, and his brocade dressing gown was of a shade of mauve that did absolutely nothing to enhance his appearance. He looked exactly how he felt, dreadful, and his headache didn't benefit at all from the bright sunshine streaming in through the window.

Rosalind sipped only coffee, too, but her lack of appetite had nothing to do with feeling unwell. She hadn't slept at all after the ball, because she couldn't stop thinking about Philip, and thoughts of him filled her head now. She ran her fingertip around the lip of her cup, gazing at the bowl of yellow pansies in the middle of the table. Her hair was pinned up loosely into a knot on the top of her head, and she wore a pink-and-white seersucker gown, short-sleeved, with a demure neckline. A light shawl rested over her arms, slipping slightly as she bent to stroke the head of her father's favorite hound, which had somehow managed to slip into the room to hide beneath the table ready for any tidbits either she or John selected for it.

Her mother looked perplexedly at her. "Rosalind, my dear, are you feeling quite well this morning?"

"Yes, quite well, thank you."

"You haven't eaten anything."

"I'm not very hungry, that's all." Rosalind flushed a little guiltily, for she knew that she'd soon have to tell them that there wouldn't be a match with George Whitby, and why.

Mr. Carberry rustled his newspaper and then abruptly folded it, placing it on the table as he eyed his son. "It's no wonder your sister has no appetite this morning, sir; she's still recovering from having to receive that damned Englishman!"

John drew a long breath, but didn't reply. He studied his cup of coffee as if it were of immense interest.

The refusal to respond antagonized Mr. Carberry into the long-awaited outburst. "I've had enough of you recently, sir, for you've been more trouble than you're worth," he snapped.

Mrs. Carberry sat quickly forward in a whisper of dove-gray taffeta, her eyes anxious. "Please, William, there's no need . . ."

"On the contrary, my dear, there's every need. We've tried sweet reason, and we've tried endless patience, but it's all to no avail." He fixed his gaze upon John again. "You've been wallowing in self-pity for more than a year now, and it's got to stop. Your wild ways brought about the death of the woman you loved, and nothing can change that."

John's green eyes flashed toward him. "I'm well aware of that fact, sir," he replied stiffly.

"Are you also aware that behaving the way you do isn't going to bring her back?"

"I won't dignify that question with an answer," answered

John shortly, his eyes no longer lackluster, but very bright and angry.

"And what would you know of dignity, sir?" demanded Mr. Carberry relentlessly. "What dignity is there in staggering home night after night in your cups? What dignity is there in losing heavily at the gaming tables? And what dignity is there in foisting your damned Englishman upon us all at a Fourth of July ball? Your little prank ruined the evening, and I find that unforgivable!"

"Philip's presence hardly constituted the ruining of the evening," retorted John.

"Not in your eyes, maybe, but then your standards have slipped somewhat of late, haven't they? Well, I'm not about to put up with your base conduct any longer. It's time you came to terms with Elizabeth's death, and unless you do, you can look elsewhere for a roof over your head. Do I make myself clear?"

"You do, sir," John replied in a clipped tone.

"I expect to see an improvement straightaway, sir. Straightaway."

Witout another word, John tossed his napkin on the table and strode out. The hound slipped from its hiding place beneath the table to follow him. Its paws pattered on the polished floorboards and then the door closed.

Mrs. Carberry looked reproachfully at her husband. "Was there any need to be quite so unkind, William?" she asked.

"He needed a plain talking-to, my dear, it was long overdue." He picked up his newspaper again, rustling it noisily as he made much of selecting a certain page.

Mrs. Carberry exchanged a glance with Rosalind, and then said nothing more.

Rosalind wanted to go to John, for she knew how desperately keen his grief over Elizabeth still was, but rushing after him now would only make matters worse as far as her father was concerned.

Her mother looked at her. "What do you intend to do this morning, my dear? Is George calling on you?"

"No, he isn't. Actually, I thought I'd go for a ride."

"A ride? Rosalind, when are you going to give George an answer?"

Rosalind hesitated. "I already have, Mother."

Mrs. Carberry gasped. "You have? Oh, my dear . . ."

"I've declined him, Mother," Rosalind went on quietly.

Her mother stared at her, and Mr. Carberry put down his newspaper for a second time.

"You've what?" he demanded.

"I've declined George's proposal."

"May I ask why?"

The time wasn't right to tell them about Philip. "I'm just not in love with him, Father."

"Love? What has love got to do with marriage?"

"A great deal, as far as I'm concerned."

"It's never been mentioned as a criterion before," he said, "and if it's so important, why have you waited until now to say anything?"

"I—I didn't realize it was so important to me before, Father."

He sighed and sat back in his chair. "You do know what a good match you've turned down, don't you?"

"Yes."

"George Whitby is heir to—"

"I know, Father, and I'm sorry. I know you wanted the match to come about, and I truly meant to go through with it, but now I just can't. I want to marry for love, not just for fondness and regard."

"Fondess and regard were good enough for your mother and me."

Rosalind fell silent, for until Philip de Grey it had been good enough for her, too.

Her mother studied her. "Is your mind made up on this, my dear?"

"Yes."

"Then there's nothing more to be said. We're disappointed, of course, but the times have long since gone when parents forced their daughters into unwanted marriages.''

Rosalind smiled gratefully at her for not pushing the matter, but for several minutes afterward she could feel her pensive glances. Did her mother suspect a little of the truth?

Mr. Carberry excused himself from the breakfast table shortly after that, declaring himself to be thoroughly displeased with both his children. As the door closed behind him, Rosalind expected her mother to say something, but she didn't. Several minutes later it was time to change for the ride.

Her maid was waiting. Hetty was a competent, flaxen-haired young woman with a shy smile and china-blue eyes, and she spoke with only a slight hint of her Viennese origins, having lived in America for the last ten years. She'd been Rosalind's maid for three of those ten years, and knew her well enough to guess that a momentous event of some sort had happened. Usually Rosalind would have confided in the maid, but not this time; it was all too private and important to be shared with anyone except Philip himself.

Hetty brought the emerald-green riding habit and laid it gently on the pink silk coverlet of the bed. A few minutes later Rosalind was ready to leave. She studied her reflection in the gilt-framed cheval glass. As she drew on her gloves, she was conscious of a quiver of nervous anticipation. Would it still be the same this morning when she met Philip? Would the magic of the night before seize them both again? Or would the clear light of day make all the difference in the world? She stared at her image. Maybe for him it already had made all the difference in the world, and he wouldn't even keep the assignation.

She heard her horse being led around to the front of the house, and Hetty quickly brought her her riding crop. Then she left the room, but as she reached the top of the staircase, she halted in dismay, for John was waiting for her in the entrance hall below, and he was dressed for riding.

He was leaning back against a console table, his arms folded and his eyes downcast thoughtfully. He wore a maroon riding jacket and beige cord breeches, and his top hat, gloves, and riding crop lay on the table beside him.

Hearing her at the top of the staircase, he glanced up and straightened. "I heard you ordering your horse earlier and thought I might join you."

"I'm not doing anything exciting," she replied, injecting what she hoped was just the right note of discouragement into her voice.

"My nerves are too ragged for excitement."

She gave a weak smile and went slowly down, wishing she could think of something to deter him.

He watched her. "At the risk of sounding boringly repetitive, I have to say yet again that you look quite delectable. George will be the envy of Washington with you as his wife."

She was about to tell him she wasn't going to be George's wife, but he turned away to pick up his top hat and tap it on. Then he donned his gloves, picked up his riding crop, and offered her his arm. "Shall we go?"

They went out into the sunshine, and as John assisted her to mount, she turned to look at him. "I'm sure you have other things you'd much rather do than ride with me . . ."

"Don't you want my company?"

"Yes, of course, it's just . . ."

"I'm looking forward to riding with you, Sis, so don't say anything more." He grinned, patting her arm before turning to take the reins of his own horse, which had been led out with hers.

She sighed inwardly. The last thing she wanted was company, but there was very little she could do about it. She and John had always been allies in the past, but would he be her ally in this?

They rode down the freshly raked drive toward the gates. Washington gleamed across the marshland, where cattle moved between the clumps of alders. Someone was shooting partridge, and the gun reports cracked sharply through the warm, still air. There were clouds on the distant horizon,

and she knew there'd be a thunderstorm before night-
fall.

The horses kickedup dust as they were urged along the
track toward the wooden hillside that rose to the east of the
mansion, and the suddenness of their approach startled a
magpie from a bush. With loud cries of alarm, it flapped
into the nearest tree, where it sat in angry indignation, its
chattering complaints ringing after them as they rode into
the cool shade of the woods.

Rosalind tried to think of suitable ways to mention Philip,
but it soon became apparent that John was accompanying
her in order to talk about his own problem. They rode slowly
between the trees, where leafy shadows moved across their
path, and he spoke at length about all he'd lost when Elizabeth
had died.

Rosalind reined in after a while. "Elizabeth wouldn't have
wanted you to stay unhappy because of her, John," she said
gently.

'It's my fault that she died.''

"Maybe it is, but Father's right, you can't go on like this.
Will you promise me something, John?''

"That depends.''

"Promise me that you'll do as Father wishes.''

"Sis . . .''

"Not for his sake, John, but for your own. You can't go
on as you have been, and I think that in your heart you know
it.''

He drew a heavy breath, tipping his top hat back
on his blond hair. "It's more easily said than done,
Rosie.''

"No, it isn't, John. You've just got to make up your mind
what you want.''

He looked shrewdly at her. "You say that as if it's something you've done yourself.''

She hesitated. "I have.''

"Are you going to explain?''

"Are you going to give me your promise?''

He smiled a little. "Very well, you have my word that I'll change my ways."

"Don't say it lightly, John."

"I'm not. I mean every word. Now, then, what is it that you've made your mind up about?"

She glanced ahead through the trees. At the top of the incline ahead was the fallen tree, where she hoped Philip would be waiting for her.

John followed the glance. "It isn't like you to be mysterious, Sis."

"Nor is it like me to be reckless to the point of lunacy, but that's exactly what I am being. John, I'm not just going for a ride this morning, I'm going to keep a tryst with Philip de Grey."

He stared at her, at first just stunned, but then angrily. "Have you taken leave of your senses?" he breathed incredulously.

'No. In fact, I've never been more certain about anything in my life."

"But, dammit, you've only met him once!"

"I know."

"And what of George?"

"He already knows."

John's lips parted in amazement. "He does?"

'He realized last night."

"How perceptive of him."

"If you hadn't been so in drink, you'd probably have realized it yourself," she replied sharply. Then she bit her lip regretfully. "I'm sorry, John, I didn't mean it to sound like that."

"I rather think you did, and I probably deserve it." He breathed in slowly. "Sis, I can't let you keep this assignation. If I do, I'll be guilty of standing idly by while you compromise yourself beyond redemption."

"Please, John," she begged.

"Rosalind, drunk or not, I'd never have brought him near the house if I'd realized this would happen."

"I must speak to him, John."

"No," he replied firmly, reaching over to seize the bridle of her horse.

"If you do this now, John Carberry, so help me I'll never forgive you. I stood by you when Elizabeth died, and I've understood your grief over her. While she was alive I did everything I could to help you pusue the match with her, even though I knew our parents wanted a more wealthy bride for you. All I'm asking of you now is that you let me meet Philip. You owe it to me."

"Damn you, Rosalind."

"You owe it to me," she said again, holding his gaze.

Slowly he released the horse. "If this was any man but Philip de Grey . . ."

"Because he's British?"

"Because he means nothing but heartbreak for you, Sis. You've called in my debt, and I'm paying it, but I hope with all my heart that this is the first and last time you have anything to do with him." He gathered his reins. "Shall we ride on?"

"I'd rather you waited here for me."

"It will do no harm for him to know that I'm now party to what's going on." He kicked his heels, urging his horse on up the hillside.

Rosalind hesitated for a moment, and then rode after him.

4

To her relief, Philip was waiting by the fallen tree as he'd promised. He'd dismounted from his large and rather restive black horse, and was leaning back against the tree trunk, the reins swinging idly in his gloved hand as he gazed at the magnificent view toward Washington. He wore an indigo riding coat and cream kerseymere breeches that fitted him like a second skin. There was no starch in his full muslin neckcloth, so that the folds moved slightly as a stray breeze stirred lazily through the hitherto still air. He'd hung his top hat on a branch, and the sunlight fell fully on his coal-black hair as he straightened on seeing their approach.

He tethered his horse and then came toward them. The smile on his lips faded perceptibly as he saw John's anger, and after giving Rosalind the briefest but warmest of glances, it was to John that he gave his full attention.

Rosalind reined in unhappily, for she knew that John intended to confront Philip on her account and there was nothing she could do to prevent him.

Philip surveyed him, his blue eyes cool and guarded. "It's evident that you have something disagreeable to say."

"Are you surprised?"

"No. In your place I'd feel as you do."

"Would you treat a London lady of quality in this way?

Would you compromise her without a second thought?''

"I do not seek to compromise Rosalind.''

"Then what do you seek?''

"My intentions are honorable, and that, I think, is all you need to know.''

"Don't adopt that lofty English tone with me, damn you,'' snapped John, his green eyes bright with affront. "You've known my sister for less than a day, and you've somehow persuaded her to keep this unbelievably rash tryst with you. Don't preach to me about honorable intentions, for we both know that that simply isn't so.''

"Do we indeed?'' Philip murmured softly. "You seem to be very sure about 'our' thoughts.''

"Perhaps because you and I nearly met the day before yesterday.''

Rosalind looked quickly at her brother, wondering what he was leading up to.

Philip's gaze remained steady. "And what has that got to do with it? We didn't meet until yesterday, and I know full well that I haven't shared any thoughts concerning Rosalind with you.''

"I'll tell you what it's got to do with it, Southvale. I overheard you in a very interesting conversation with your envoy. Do you perhaps recall the conversation I'm referring to?''

"No, I'm afraid I don't.''

"It was at the Hardiston house. You and he were in the billiard room.''

A light passed through Philip's eyes, and he nodded. "Yes, I recall the occasion.''

"Not being a war hawk by inclination, I intended to make myself agreeable to you both, but as I was about to go into the room, I realized that your conversation was of a rather private nature.''

Philip drew a long breath, glancing at Rosalind. "Yes, it was,'' he admitted.

John leaned forward on the pommel of his saddle in a challenging manner. "Shall I repeat what I heard, or would you prefer to say it yourself?"

"I'm quite prepared to speak for myself, although I cannot promise to use the exact words." Philip looked steadily at him for a moment and then turned to Rosalind. "What John overheard, I believe, was my somewhat emotional declaration that I still loved my wife, that there wasn't a moment of any day when I didn't think of her, and that I wished with all my heart that she was still with me. I meant every word."

Her heart tightened within her, and she remembered George's parting words of warning at the ball, when he'd said that there were many obstacles between her and a man like Philip, not the least of those obstacles being Philip's enduring love for his wife.

John gave a savage half-laugh. "There speaks the man of honorable intentions! I said he'd mean nothing but heartbreak for you, Sis, and now perhaps you understand why. You're nothing more than a fleeting diversion for him, and your seduction is just a pleasant way for him to idle away his time."

Philip rounded on him, his lips thin and cold. "Take those words back, Carberry, or so help me, I'll call you out!"

Rosalind's breath caught in alarm. "Please, Philip . . ."

His attention was still upon John. "I asked you to take those words back, Carberry, and I'm still waiting for you to do it."

"I have nothing to take back, Southvale."

Rosalind dismounted, hurrying to stand between them. "Please stop this right now," she cried, snatching John's horse's bridle and making it back away slightly.

Philip's eyes were still steel-bright, but then he looked at her and his gaze softened a little. "Forgive me, Rosalind, for the last thing I wish to do is upset you. He may be your brother, but that doesn't give him the right to say what he did. I don't deny what he overheard at the Hardiston house, and as I've admitted, I meant every word. But that was then, before I met you. I wouldn't say those words now, because they've ceased to be true. You're all that matters to me now, and you have been from the very first moment I saw you."

She wanted to believe him, but was it possible for a beloved wife to fade so suddenly from her husband's heart?

He read her thoughts. "Only this time yesterday you were still inclined to marry George Whitby, were you not?"

"Yes."

"But all that changed quite suddenly, didn't it?"

"Yes."

"Because of me?"

"Yes," she whispered.

"Then is it so beyond belief that I, too, could undergo such a change of heart?"

Slowly she shook her head, returning the smile. "No, it isn't."

John looked urgently at her. "Use your head, Rosalind! Don't let him—"

Philip stepped over to him, snatching his reins. "Your concern for your sister does you immense credit, Carberry, but quite frankly, I'm astonished by your total lack of understanding."

"Oh, I understand only too well!"

"No, sir, you don't. I'm not attempting to seduce Rosalind, and she's certainly far more to me than a passing fancy. I would expect you, of all men, to understand how I feel right now."

"Why me?"

"Because from what I've heard about you, you're a man much governed by his heart."

John met his eyes, but said nothing.

Philip still held the reins. "Washington chitter-chatter has much to say about you, Carberry. It seems that your conduct in recent months has been less than dignified."

"Have a care, Southvale . . ."

"I intend to say my piece, just as you took it upon yourself to say yours. You loved and lost, and now you're consumed with grief. I sympathize, believe me, for I've been where you are now, but there is one signal difference between you and me, and that is that I would never *ever* brush aside as meaningless the feelings of others, least of all my own sister."

"Do you have a sister?"

"Yes, and I love her very much. I would never belittle her as you're belittling Rosalind."

John stiffened. "I'm not belittling—"

"That's exactly what you're doing. Does Rosalind make a habit of inviting the attentions of the opposite sex? Does she have a reputation here in Washington?"

"No, damn it!"

"Is this the first time she's done anything like this?"

"Yes."

"Then surely it stands to reason that she must have good reason for behaving in a way that's so out of character?"

John exhaled slowly, his eyes moving to Rosalind as he nodded. "Yes, I suppose she must have," he conceded unwillingly.

"My intentions are honorable—indeed, they couldn't be more honorable—and all I ask is that you allow us a little time together now. You have my word that she will come to no harm at my hands."

For a long moment John hesitated, but then he nodded again. "Very well."

"Thank you."

"But if you cause her a moment's hurt, you'll have me to deal with."

"And I will deserve it."

John looked at Rosalind, then turned his horse. "I'll wait at the edge of the woods." He kicked his heels and rode away.

Philip turned to Rosalind, gently taking her hands. "Do you regret coming here today?" he asked softly.

"No," she whispered.

He smiled, pulling her closer. His arm slipped around her waist, and she moved into his embrace as if she'd done so a thousand times before. He held her for a long moment and then tilted her face toward his, kissing her slowly and luxuriously on the lips.

A rich and heady desire stirred through her, and she felt as if she were awakening from a long and deep slumber. The desire increased, becoming an exhilarating passion, and a soft moan escaped her as she linked her arms around his neck to return the kiss. Her body ached for him, and her skin tingled at his touch; she felt warm and weightless, alive only for him, and she knew that a craving had been aroused that would only be slaked by complete submission to this one man. There was nothing hesitant or uncertain about her feelings, they were vibrant and clear. She loved him, in less than a day she loved him, and it was a love that would never falter.

He drew away, cupping her face in his hands. His blue eyes were dark and his voice low with feeling. "You know that I love you, don't you?"

A wild joy swept through her and tears filled her eyes. "Yes, I know, because I love you too."

"I meant what I said when John was here. I did say those things he overheard, but Celia truly became the past for me when I saw you. I removed my wedding ring before I left for the ball, and I know that I will never wear it again."

"Did you love her very much?"

"Yes."

"What was she like?" she asked suddenly.

"Do you really want to know about her?"

"Yes, Philip, because she possessed you first. She shared your life, your love, and your bed, and I want desperately to know about her."

"You have no need to fear her, for it's you I love now."

"Please tell me."

He exhaled slowly and nodded. "Very well. She was very beautiful indeed, with dark curls, lilac eyes, and a heart-shaped face. She was petite, witty, vivacious, and totally fascinating. Men were drawn to her like moths to a flame, she was the belle of London society, and of all the many suitors who sought her hand, I was the one upon whom she bestowed her favor. We were married for only two years before she died, and to my eternal regret we parted that last time on a sour note."

"You'd quarreled?"

"Not quarreled, exactly, but we'd certainly disagreed. As you now know, I have a sister. Her name is Katherine, she lives with me, and she and I are very close. At about the time Celia decided to go on yet another of her many trips to visit her family in Ireland, Katherine's hopes of marrying the man she loved came to an abrupt and cruel end when he deserted her to marry someone else. Katherine was distraught, and although I tried my best to offer her comfort and sympathy, it was the understanding of another woman she really needed. My great-aunt, Lady Eleanor Laird, who also resides with us, happened to be away in Scotland at the time, and so there was only Celia for Katherine to turn to. But Celia refused to even delay her visit to Ireland, even though I specifically asked her to, for Katherine's sake. We therefore parted a little acrimoniously, and word reached me a week later that her ship had foundered on rocks off the Irish coast." He looked away, falling silent.

Rosalind slipped her hand into his.

His fingers closed over hers. "I was in despair, distraught with grief, and I didn't think I'd ever get over it. Ironically, it was Katherine, so unhappy herself, who gave me the comfort and understanding I needed. She knew I needed something to take my mind off my loss, and she urged me to return to my diplomatic interests. It was because of her that I roused myself to take the assignment in St. Petersburg, and because of her that my name was put forward at the last moment to come here.''

"Then I have much to thank her for," Rosalind said softly.

He smiled. "We both have much to thank her for."

"What is your life like in London?"

"Privileged, in a word."

"Tell me about it."

"At the risk of boring you?"

"I want to know all about you."

He raised her hand to his lips. "Then I'll tell you whatever you wish to know. My title and family go back into the mists of time, and I have many responsibilities as landlord of a great estate five miles outside London, owner of woolen mills in the Cotswolds, tin mines in the north of Cornwall, shipping interests in Falmouth, in the south of the same county, and various other commercial dealings in the City of London. I have a town residence in St. James's, overlooking Green Park, and I keep saddle horses that are the envy of many a sporting gentleman. My racehorses have managed to win me the Derby on two occasions, and the Ascot Gold Cup once, and I have a cutter, the *Lady Eleanor*, that I race on the Thames estuary. I'm usually to be found on the best guest lists—at least I was until a year ago—and I am known in royal circles. I am a friend of the Prince of Wales, or rather the Prince Regent, as he's been for the past few months, and I have often stayed with him at Carlton House. I ride in Hyde Park, have private boxes at both the Theatre Royal and the Italian Opera House, belong to several of the more exclusive clubs, and can always gain entry to Almack's." He smiled into her eyes. "Will that do? Or do you wish to know still more?"

"I think that will do. You're right, your life is indeed privileged."

"Yours is hardly deprived."

"That's true. Is there anything you wish to know about me?"

His eyes moved tenderly over her face. "I found out all I needed to before I met you yesterday. Rosalind . . ."

"Yes?"

"Last night I told you that I might be sent back to London at any time."

Dismay leapt through her. "Have you heard something? Is there going to be war?"

His fingers tightened reassuringly over hers. "No, I haven't heard anything. As to whether there will be war, I have to say that I fear there will be."

"You seem very sure."

"I can't see that there's any alternative. America is determined to protect her freedom and right to trade as she chooses, which includes trading with France, but Britain is fighting for her very life against Bonaparte, and thus cannot possibly stand by and allow that French trade to continue. Don't misunderstand me, for I'm not attempting to sanctify the British. I know we're at fault, we treat the high seas as if we own them, we stop your shipping, impress your seamen, blockade your shores, and generally behave as if you're still our colony. But you're *not* still our colony, you're an independent nation now, and the last thing you're going to do is bow to arrogant British demands. The last thing Britain is going to do is let you get on with it at present, and so, yes, I fear war is inevitable, with the only benefactor being Bonaparte, who must be hugging himself with joy at the way things are going.

She lowered her eyes. "War will separate us, Philip."

"Rosalind, I told John that my intentions toward you were honorable, that they couldn't be more honorable, and that's exactly what they are. I want you to be my wife, to become the second Lady Southvale, and to come back to England with me."

She stared at him. "Your wife?" she whispered.

"Do you imagine I could be satisfied with anything less? I love you, Rosalind, and have done so from the very first moment I saw you. Events have moved so swiftly that I can scarce believe they've happened, but of one thing there can be no doubt at all. You mean everything to me, and I can't envisage returning to England without you." He drew her fingertips to his lips again. "I know I'm asking a great deal of you, not only to marry me so quickly, but also to leave your home and come halfway across the world, but I still ask you. Will you be my wife?"

"Philip . . ."

"Marry me, Rosalind," he pressed softly.

His voice caressed her, and caution slipped away into the warm air. She smiled. "Yes, Philip, I'll marry you."

5

It was another warm, humid evening two days later when Mr. Carberry reluctantly prepared to receive Philip in the library at the mansion. From the window he could see the rose garden, where Rosalind and her mother waited anxiously in the summerhouse for the outcome of what was bound to be a difficult meeting.

Mr. Carberry sighed, for his wife was resigned to the match, having perceived the way things were going from the moment Rosalind had declared that nothing less than a love match would do. John wasn't in favor of Philip de Grey as a brother-in-law, he'd made that clear enough, and his reason was the same as his worried father's: Philip's recent and well-known grief over his first wife was just that, too recent and well-known. It would be far, far better if things could be postponed, so that the first Lady Southvale had indeed ceased to matter, and that was how Mr. Carberry intended to conduct the interview.

He waited by the window, gazing across the marsh toward Washington. He'd be civil enough, but if he had his way, Philip de Grey would depart after agreeing to indefinitely postpone any thought of a formal betrothal, and certainly any thought of an early wedding. He sighed heavily, for Rosalind had always been a dutiful daughter, but the advent of this damned Englishman had changed all that. For the first time she'd made it plain that for Philip de Grey, she was prepared to defy her father.

Steps approached the library door, and Mr. Carberry turned, automatically straightening his cravat and charcoal-and-white-striped coat.

Philip was announced, and came in, bowing respectfully. Mr. Carberry's critical glance raked him from head to toe, taking in the stylish fawn coat, brown brocade waistcoat, cream breeches, and frilled shirt. The fellow knew a thing or two about sartorial matters, that was for sure, and had the sort of looks that attracted the female sex like pins to a magnet.

A rather embarrassed silence hung for a moment, and then Philip spoke. "Thank you for receiving me, sir."

"When my daughter's happiness is at stake, I don't have much choice."

"Rosalind's happiness is my only concern as well, sir," replied Philip quietly.

"Is it? If you'll forgive me for saying so, Lord Southvale, the speed with which you've moved so far can't have given you much time to consider anything with any depth." Mr. Carberry pressed his lips together, not wanting to allow his natural antagonism toward this man get the better of him. He'd promised Rosalind and her mother that he'd be courteous, and courteous was what he'd damned well be. "May I offer you a glass of cognac, sir?"

"Thank you."

The decanter clinked against the glasses, and then Mr. Carberry gave one to Philip, before indicating a chair by the fireplace. "Please be seated, sir, for I see no reason why we should not be comfortable while we speak."

Philip did as he was bade, and Mr. Carberry sat opposite him.

"Lord Southvale, I cannot pretend to welcome what's happened."

"I didn't expect that you would, sir."

"Indeed?" Mr. Carberry raised an eyebrow.

"If I were in your place, sir, I'd be displeased as well. I'm hardly likely to be your notion of an ideal choice, am I?" A faint smile touched Philip's lips.

"No, sir, you're not, but if I'm completely honest, your unsuitability arises from your feelings toward your first wife, and not from anything else. Forgive me for speaking plainly upon a matter that is private to you, but you must understand my anxiety."

"It's clear that John has repeated to you what he overheard at the Hardiston house."

"Yes."

"I don't pretend I didn't say those things, but I do deny that they are of any significance now."

"Because you glanced out of a window and saw my daughter drive past?"

"Yes."

Mr. Carberry gave a slight laugh. "I'm sorry, Lord Southvale, but I find that very hard to believe. Perhaps it's because I'm not of a romantic disposition." He swirled his cognac, sniffing the bouquet. "Love matches are an unknown quantity to me, sir, since my marriage was arranged before my wife and I had ever met."

"But you've nevertheless been very happy?"

Mr. Carberry nodded. "Yes."

"Can you envisage life without Mrs. Carberry?" Philip asked quietly.

Rosalind's father paused. "No, I don't think I can."

"Nor can I envisage life without Rosalind."

Mr. Carberry surveyed him for a long moment and then sipped the cognac. "I understand from Rosalind that there are two ladies who reside in your household, your sister and your aunt?"

"Great-aunt. Yes, sir, my sister, Katherine, is unmarried and lives with me, and my widowed great-aunt, Lady Eleanor Laird, acts in the capacity of chaperone."

"I've no doubt that they will be as shocked by your whirlwind romance as I've been."

Philip smiled a little. "It will startle them, yes, but they will make Rosalind very welcome."

"If she leaves here," qualified Mr. Carberry.

"Of course."

"What if they don't welcome her?"

"Then they are the ones whose position will be difficult, because Rosalind will be Lady Southvale, mistress of the house, and I will uphold her in every way. But the problem is hypothetical, for I know them both very well and am quite content that they will be glad about her."

"Glad about an American Lady Southvale when war is in the air?"

"Mr. Carberry, London society hasn't set its face against America; indeed, I think you'll find a little more hostility against the British here in Washington than you'll find vice versa in London."

Mr. Carberry drew a long breath. "You're probably right. We're still a young nation, sir, and fiercely proud of our hard-won independence."

"Independence from the British yoke," murmured Philip dryly.

Mr. Carberry smiled. "Precisely, sir."

"I don't intend to impose my will upon Rosalind. What I propose is an alliance of the very highest order. I love her, and I want to cherish her, always."

"Pretty words, Lord Southvale."

"Truthful words, Mr. Carberry."

Rosalind's father nodded. "Yes, sir, I think they probably are."

"I'm relieved to have convinced you of that."

Mr. Carberry rose to his feet. "What you haven't convinced me, however, is that there's any need for the haste you both seem set upon."

"I may be sent back to London at any moment."

"Yes, I know. I also know that in the new year you expect to go to St. Petersburg, which means that Rosalind will be left alone in London."

"Hardly alone, sir, she'll be with my sister and great-aunt. And besides, I'll be away only for a few months."

Mr. Carberry chose his words carefully. "It seems to me that it would be better all around if you waited until after St. Petersburg, and then came back here to marry, if you and Rosalind are still so inclined."

Philip's blue eyes rested closely upon him. "Are you counseling a delay because you feel it would be sensible and more becoming, or because you hope in your heart that in the meantime Rosalind will change her mind about me?"

Mr. Carberry turned. "If you want the truth, I have to admit that at the outset of the interview the latter was indeed the case. I was extremely cynical about an affair of such short duration, and I didn't want Rosalind to enter a marriage that would take her so far away from her home, family, and friends. But you've impressed me, Lord Southvale, and I accept that I must bow to the inevitable, or lose my daughter."

The light of relief passed through Philip's eyes. Permission was going to be given.

"However," went on Rosalind's father, "I am determined to protect her reputation, and so must insist that matters proceed from now on in a very proper way. I'm not suggesting that impropriety of any kind has already taken place," he added quickly, "it's just that such a hasty betrothal and marriage is bound to cause talk that will tarnish Rosalind's name."

"I respect your point, sir, but there is something else that has to be considered."

"And that is?"

"That if we wait until after my return from St. Petersburg, war will in all probability have broken out between our two countries, and that will mean an indefinite postponement."

"War may yet be diverted."

"I fear it won't be, for both sides appear to be intransigent."

Mr. Carberry drew a long breath and then nodded regretfully. "There is a certain inevitability about it, I have to admit," he said quietly. "Very well, I concede that such a long wait is out of the question, but I'm still concerned that unwelcome comment will arise if the wedding takes place too quickly. I understand from Rosalind that you both wish the marriage to take place as quickly as possible, maybe even before July is out."

"Yes, because I could suddenly have to go back to London."

"But it's true, is it not, that you could be here for many months yet?"

"Whether or not there are any developments in the talks, I'll still have to be in England again by Christmas, because I have to receive detailed instructions prior to leaving for Russia in the new year."

"I understand your feeling of urgency, but I'm afraid July is unacceptably soon when it's very doubtful that you will have to leave so quickly. Politicians always have a great deal of hot air to expel before they resort to broadsides, and so I suggest a compromise."

"A compromise?"

"Rosalind's twenty-third birthday is at the end of August, and that would seem to me to be a suitable date to choose. Eight weeks or so, that's all I ask, and at the end of it there will be a wedding that Washington will talk of with admiration for years to come. Will you agree to that?"

Philip wished he could feel as confident that the talks wouldn't yield anything within the next eight weeks, but he could see that Mr. Carberry had made his mind up on the matter. It was important to Rosalind that she have her parents' blessing, although she was prepared to defy them if necessary, but was the possibility of an early return to London worth the risk of a family rift that would undoubtedly cause her unhappiness in the future? No, it wasn't. Putting his glass down, he smiled and rose to his feet, his hand extended.

"You have my agreement, sir," he said.

The handshake was warm, for both men liked and respected each other far more than either of them had expected at the commencement of the meeting.

Mr. Carberry then glanced out of the window. "I think it's time to tell the ladies, don't you?"

They left the library, going quickly through the house to the terrace, but as Mr. Carberry walked on down the wide stone steps and along the rose-garden path, Philip was suddenly accosted by John, who emerged from the French windows of the ballroom.

"A word with you, Southvale."

Philip paused, his blue eyes cool as he turned to face Rosalind's brother. John had remained hostile ever since they'd had the confrontation in the wood, and his manner now did not suggest a change of heart.

John halted before him. "The cordiality between you and my father suggests that you've won him around."

"He's given his consent, yes."

"Well, you haven't won me around."

"I'm well aware of that," replied Philip levelly.

"I don't believe you're over your first wife, and I know you're going to make my sister unhappy. When that happens, I'll tear you limb from limb, do you hear?"

"I hear."

"Don't ever forget." John turned on his heel, walking quickly away.

Philip watched him for a moment and then went on down the steps to the rose garden.

Mr. Carberry had already reached the summerhouse and had broken the news. Rosalind was running joyfully along the path, the white satin ribbons in her hair fluttering prettily. She wore a pale-yellow lawn gown, flounced and frilled, and there were pearls at her throat. Immeasurable happiness shone in her green eyes as she flung herself into Philip's arms. She was too overcome to speak, and he held her close, his fingers curling in the warm hair at the nape of her neck. Her body was lithe and slender, and he could feel her heart beating close to his. Her perfume filled his nostrils, essence of the roses after which she was called.

He buried his face against her golden hair, closing his eyes as he whispered her name.

6

Washington society was startled by the sudden betrothal announcement, for everyone had expected Rosalind to marry George Whitby, not an English lord who hadn't been in America for more than a week. The war hawks in the capital were thoroughly disapproving, for a man like Philip was anathema to them at the moment, but most of the Carberrys' friends and acquaintances soon came around to the match. There was, as Mr. Carberry had predicted, a certain amount of unwelcome speculation as to the real reason for such haste, but in general it was accepted that the political situation was behind it. The romance and magic of love at first sight captured society's imagination, and the wedding at the end of August was an event that was soon looked forward to with much anticipation. Elegant social occasions were always popular in Washington's best circles, and the day that Rosalind Carberry became the second Lady Southvale promised to be a highlight of the year.

George continued to be gracious in defeat, for which Rosalind felt she was much in his debt. He could so easily have taken umbrage, but instead was magnanimous, taking great care to remain on friendly terms with the entire Carberry family. John remained obdurate about the match, although he was loyal enough in public, for Rosalind's sake.

Privately, however, he left her in no doubt that he still disliked the situation. Nothing would convince him that Philip really was over Celia Beaufort, and because of this, he saw only distress ahead for Rosalind.

While preparations for the wedding got under way, the talks continued between Mr. Foster and the American government, but there didn't seem to be any hope of a settlement of the two countries' great differences. America's insistence upon trading with France was an unacceptable state of affairs for Britain, and Britain's determined interference was an insuperable obstacle for America, who saw no reason why she should not trade with whichever foreign nation she chose.

The royal navy's blockade of the eastern seaboard continued, and there were a number of skirmishes that incited a great deal of public indignation in America, but although the situation worsened, it didn't topple over into the war that lay in waiting.

Rosalind tried not to think of the outbreak of armed conflict. She threw herself into the wedding preparations, assisting her mother to compile lists, decide upon the great feast that was to take place in the ballroom, and choose the flowers. Then there was the small matter of her wedding gown, a dazzling confection of diaphanous white silk, silver tissue, and tiny embroidered pearls that promised to make her one of the loveliest brides Washington had ever seen.

July gave way to August, and the weather became hotter and even more humid. The days slid by, and the wedding came closer and closer. It seemed that nothing was going to ruin all the carefully laid plans, but then, only three days before the ceremony, fate harshly intervened. Mr. Foster's talks with President Madison and Secretary of State Monroe suddenly yielded an important development, and the envoy immediately realized that it was of such significance that he could not make a decision without instructions from London. He had no choice but to ask Philip to return there at once, and at less than two hours' notice. HMS *Minerva* was waiting at Annapolis and would sail the moment Philip was on board.

There was barely time for Philip to ride to the mansion to tell Rosalind what had happened, and as he dismounted at the door, he knew that what he had to tell her would break her heart.

She was just coming down the staircase, having seen him ride up the drive. She was in a carefree mood, looking fresh and dainty in a peach-and-white-checkered muslin gown, her hair tied lightly back with a wide brown ribbon. The glad smile died on her lips as she saw his serious expression.

"Philip? What is it?"

He tossed his top hat and gloves on a table and then hurried to meet her at the foot of the staircase. "Are your parents in?"

"No, they're attending a reception at the White House. John's out riding with some friends." She searched his face. "Something's very wrong, isn't it?"

He took her hands, his thumbs pressing her palms. "There isn't an easy way to say this, Rosalind. I have to leave immediately for London."

She stared numbly at him. "No," she whispered, "please let this be a bad dream . . ."

"It's no dream, my darling. HMS *Minerva* is waiting at Annapolis and will sail the moment I'm aboard."

"What's happened?"

"A development in the talks. It may be something, and it may be nothing at all, but I have to go back for further instructions. It seems your government doesn't wish to enter into a war with Britain, and is prepared to accept London's promise to rescind certain orders."

"In only a few more days we'd have been married," she said, her voice catching.

Her distress moved him, and he put his hand lovingly to her pale cheek. "If I could change this and stay, believe me, I would."

"I know." Her tear-filled green eyes moved urgently to his face. "Let me come with you now."

"No, Rosalind, for that wouldn't be right."

"Please, Philip."

"There are others to be considered in this, not just you and me."

"My family?"

"Yes."

"If my family hadn't insisted upon waiting, we'd have been married by now," she began accusingly, but then she lowered her eyes ashamedly. "I didn't mean that."

"I know."

She sought her handkerchief in her sleeve. "I can't believe fate is being this cruel."

He pulled her close, resting his head against her hair. The warm scent of roses enveloped him.

"Philip, it may be more than a year before we see each other again."

"Not necessarily."

She drew back, looking quickly at him. "What do you mean?"

"We could still be married by Christmas, but in London, not Washington."

"London?"

He held her eyes urgently. "I can't come back here, because I have to go to St. Petersburg in January, but there's no reason why you shouldn't come to me in London. And your family, too, of course. They could stay for the wedding, see all the sights, enjoy my family's hospitality, and then return here when they're satisfied that you're settled and happy."

New hope lit her eyes. "Oh, Philip . . ."

"A Christmas wedding at St. George's, Hanover Square. How does that sound?"

"It sounds quite wonderful," she breathed.

"I know your father has important business in Boston next month, and in New York for about two weeks at the beginning of October, but there's no reason why you shouldn't leave here shortly after that. The voyage to

Falmouth usually takes about four weeks, which means you could be in London toward the end of November or the beginning of December.'' He cupped her face in his hands. ''Do you think your parents will agree?''

''I'm sure I can persuade them.''

He smiled. ''Yes, I'm sure you can, too. So you'll come?''

''For a Christmas wedding in London? Yes.'' It wasn't the same as a Washington wedding in three days' time, but it was infinitely better than a ceremony some indeterminate time in the future.

He brushed his lips over hers. ''I'll write to you the moment I arrive at the Black Horse.''

''The Black Horse?''

''The inn I always use in Falmouth. Its landlord is an old friend of mine, and so I make a point of staying there whenever my shipping interests require my personal attention. Celia stayed there too, except for that last time . . .'' He broke off. ''Forgive me, for now isn't the time to mention my first wife.''

''It's going to happen, though, isn't it, so I must either get used to it or make myself wretched with jealousy.''

''You must never be jealous of the past, my darling, for it doesn't matter anymore. All that matters is the future.'' He hesitated and then took the signet ring from his finger, pressing it into her hand. ''It will be a few months more before you wear my wedding ring, but this is a token of my love.''

She began to protest. ''I can't possibly wear it, Philip, it's a family heirloom . . .''

''Please take it.'' He slipped it onto the fourth finger of her left hand, and then closed her hand, as if to prevent her from removing the ring again. ''I love you with all my heart, and nothing is going to stop me making you my wife.''

The long-case clock in the drawing room on the floor above them began to chime, the sound drifting gently to where they stood. He looked sadly into her eyes. ''I have to go now.''

With a choked sob, she flung her arms around him again,

and the tears she'd struggled to hold back for so long now
had their way. She could barely speak. "I love you too,
Philip," she whispered.

He kissed her for a last time. Her lips trembled beneath
his, and he could taste the salt of her tears. For a long moment
he couldn't bring himself to leave her, but at last he untwined
her arms, turning to snatch up his top hat and gloves and
stride from the house.

She broke down in misery, and through her sobs she heard
him riding swiftly away down the drive.

News of Lord Southvale's sudden departure spread swiftly
through Washington, and society was torn between disappointment at being denied the diversion of the wedding,
and tentative hope that Philip's mission to London might yield
something politically beneficial.

There were times during the succeeding days and weeks
when Rosalind didn't think she'd be able to endure. She was
utterly disconsolate without Philip, and although she did her
best to put on a brave face during the days, her nights were
spent weeping into her pillow.

Her parents hadn't needed a great deal of persuading about
the London wedding, and it was arranged that they'd sail
for Falmouth on the *Baltimore Lady*, a packet that was due
to sail at the beginning of the last week in October, when
Rosalind's father's various business commitments would be
over and done with.

John, however, decided not to join them in London. He
couldn't hide his relief that Philip had gone, and still made
it clear that he thought the match very ill-advised. He couldn't
shake off his deep unease about Philip's apparent sudden
turnabout concerning his first marriage, for it was John's
unhappy experience that one didn't love one person one day
and another the next. His own grief over Elizabeth hadn't
faded at all, and thus Philip's conduct was a mystery to him,
a mystery that John felt would end up costing Rosalind very
dear. Rosalind tried to understand her brother's intransigence

because she loved him so much, but there was inevitably a great deal of friction between them, and it added to the general strain of her situation as she marked off the days in her calendar.

When four weeks had passed, she hoped that the *Minerva* had reached Falmouth, but she knew it was possible that the voyage had only taken three weeks, which had been known if the winds were particularly favorable. If the winds were adverse, however, then it could be up to five weeks before land was sighted. She wouldn't know until she received the letter Philip had promised to send when he arrived at the Black Horse.

But Philip's errand to London didn't mean the marking of time politically, and incidents kept happening between American and British ships, some of them serious enough to bring renewed calls for war, no matter what. Philip had barely departed when news arrived in Washington of a particularly serious confrontation off the coast of Norfolk, when HMS *Tartarus*, while searching for deserters, had captured two American merchantmen. The *Tartarus* had then had the audacity to sail into Norfolk to restock, and it hadn't been long before a very angry crowd had gathered. The British consul was justifiably alarmed and just managed in time to scribble a hasty message to the commander of the vessel, advising him to put to sea as quickly as possible, which advice the commander prudently took. American public opinion was incensed by the incident, and Rosalind could feel the tentacles of war reaching out again.

Those tentacles seemed almost to touch her when toward the middle of September, while her father was still away in Boston, another serious incident occurred, this time when a British frigate was said to have opened fire on a defenseless American schooner, sinking her with the loss of all on board. The British denied the incident, but a passing American merchantman claimed to have witnessed everything, and there was a bitter and resentful outcry against the old enemy.

It was just after the sinking of the schooner, while Rosalind's father was still away on business, that her mother fell down the steps to the rose garden and injured her leg very badly. It was immediately apparent that she wouldn't be well enough in time to undertake the long journey to London, and Mr. Carberry returned to Washington to tell Rosalind that the wedding would have to be postponed again, until her mother was better.

Rosalind felt as if destiny was against her, for with Philip's departure for St. Petersburg in the new year, it again seemed that their marriage wouldn't take place for a long time to come.

Mr. Carberry went back to Boston to complete his business shortly afterward, and John went with him, deciding on the spur of the moment to use the opportunity to mend the continuing rift between them. Rosalind's mother was confined to her room, and a seemingly endless stream of visitors came to see her, occupying her time so fully that Rosalind was left very much to her own devices.

It was then that two things happened: Philip's promised letter arrived, and Rosalind heard about a canceled cabin on the Falmouth-bound packet *Corinth*, which was due to sail at the end of the first week in October. Philip's letter was full of love, and full of longing for their reunion by Christmas. It spoke of fair winds across the Atlantic, and his desire to reach London as quickly as possible to inform his family of his new love. Rosalind wept anew when she received it, for she knew that her reply would contain only bad news.

She didn't know at exactly what point she secretly decided to go to Philip anyway; it was just something that seemed to happen. She didn't like being deceitful, but liked even less the prospect of an indefinite separation from the man she loved so very much. Her parents would insist upon waiting, and that she would no longer do. She didn't tell anyone about her plan, except Hetty, who was to come with her, and she acquired time for herself by informing her mother she was going to stay with a friend in Baltimore.

She and the maid set off in the carriage, with only a small amount of baggage, for to have taken more would have aroused suspicions at the mansion. From the port she wrote a brief, explanatory note to her mother, begging her to forgive her and to understand why she'd taken such an enormous step. The note was sent back to Washington with the carriage, and the *Corinth* sailed on the evening tide.

The weather was fine and clear, with the crispness of early autumn in the air. A light breeze whipped tiny white crests to the waves, and the setting sun shone blood-red on the water.

Rosalind stood at the stern of the ship, watching the coast of her homeland slipping away behind the western horizon. When she could see it no more, she gathered her warm cloak around her and made her way to the bow, gazing eastward, toward Europe. She must look to the future now, and the new life that stretched before her as the second Lady Southvale.

But happiness was still going to be denied her, although she didn't know it yet, for the Philip she was running away to was a very different man from the one she'd known in Washington. Very different indeed.

7

During the early days of the voyage they sighted a number of other vessels, including several British frigates, but the *Corinth* sailed on unimpeded. They didn't witness any engagements, although one night they were awakened by the sound of cannon beyond the moonlit northern horizon.

Three days out, the weather changed and the light breeze became a fierce gale, but to the *Corinth*'s advantage. The packet pitched like a cork when the storm first began, but then was driven swiftly before the wind, soon giving Rosalind cause to hope that the crossing would only take three weeks. But if the *Corinth* fared well out of the storm, others seemed less fortunate. One day, at about the point of no return in the crossing, the lookout sighted an overturned longboat, and the captain used his telescope to make out the name on its stern. It had come from the *Queen of Falmouth*, another packet that sailed regularly between America and Britain. There was great sadness on board the *Corinth*, for there was little doubt that the other packet had foundered in the storm.

Rosalind had swiftly discovered that she was not a good sailor, and had been unwell almost from the outset of the voyage. She remained in the cabin, feeling quite dreadful, but Hetty enjoyed the sea, and was often to be found on deck. Rosalind advised her not to spend so much time in the damp, cold air, but the maid found the temptation too great and, as the voyage entered its third week, began to pay the price of her foolhardiness. By the time the lookouts had begun to search ahead for the first glimpse of the English shore and Rosalind had at last found her sea legs, Hetty had to take to her bed with high a fever.

The maid was still very ill when the lighthouse at Lizard Point shone through the gloomy evening, and Rosalind was relieved to know that by dawn they'd be in sight of Falmouth, for Hetty was in need of a doctor.

The first gray fingers of dawn reached across the sky outside and the English shore slid swiftly by on the port side. At first it was all pale and indistinct, but gradually scenery could be made out, and the colors of autumn. The wind was still very fresh and strong, but there were no clouds in the sky now, and soon the sun rose brilliantly over the eastern skyline. It was the twenty-ninth of October, and the voyage had taken just over three weeks.

Rosalind dressed in readiness to disembark as the *Corinth* slid between the twin forts guarding the entrance to Falmouth's anchorage, Carrick Roads. It was one of the finest natural harbors in the world, and a haven for many vessels, but although it was sheltered from the full force of the weather, the air was still fresh and cold. Rosalind chose warm clothes, a high-necked apricot wool gown with long sleeves, and over it she put a fur-trimmed brown velvet cloak with a hood. She did the best she could with her hair, pinning it into a reasonably adequate knot, and then she attended to Hetty, who was now far too ill to leave her bed.

Removing the maid's voluminous nightgown, Rosalind managed to dress her in a loose-fitting blue chemise gown, then she plaited the long flaxen hair so that it would stay neat. Wrapping Hetty in her warmest cloak, Rosalind left her resting on the bed and went up to the deck to see how long it would be before they could go ashore.

The rattle of the anchor chain greeted her as she emerged from the hatchway, and the *Corinth* shuddered a little. The breeze snatched at Rosalind's hood and blew playfully around her ankles as she went to stand by the rail for her first true look at England.

Carrick Roads ran more or less from south to north, a sheltered stretch of deep water that broke up inland into long creeks that fingered their way between wooded hills brilliant with the russets and golds of late October. Beyond the woods, rising in a glory of lingering purple heather and brilliant golden gorse, she could see open moorland rolling away into the heart of Cornwall.

Falmouth itself nestled against the foot of the western shore. It wasn't a beautiful town, but its importance as a port was evident in the vast number of vessels lying at anchor all around. She saw the flags of many countries, from Russia and Iceland in the north, to Turkey and Portugal in the south. Two East Indiamen were moored side by side some two hundred yards offshore, and near them she could see a brigantine and a revenue cutter. Numerous schooners, yachts, and packets were elsewhere on the sunlit water, and a whaler was just weighing anchor in the lee of the town. She saw a squadron of navy vessels, the red ensign fluttering from their masts and sterns, and she recognized the name of one corvette for it had been involved in several incidents in the blockade of New York harbor.

As she gazed at the corvette, she wondered if war had broken out at home during the past few weeks. She wondered, too, what had happened when her flight had been discovered. She felt very guilty for having run away, but Philip was the most important person in her life now, and she needed to be with him.

One of the ship's officers came to speak to her. "Begging your pardon, Miss Carberry, but the customs boat is just coming alongside, and when they've finished, the captain says he'll put the first available boat at your disposal so that you can take your maid ashore to a doctor."

"Thank you, I'm very grateful."

"Not at all, miss."

"I know we've only just arrived, but is there any way of knowing if war . . . ?"

"There's no war as yet, miss—at least, not according to the master of the *Tagus*, the Portuguese merchantman lying just over there. He was rowed just past our bow a few minutes ago, and we called down to him for news. All seems to be still well over here, but there's no way of knowing what may have happened on the other side of the Atlantic."

"No, I suppose there isn't." She looked at the shore again. A few more incidents like that with the *Tartarus* at Norfolk, and anything could have happened.

It seemed to take the customs men an age to search the ship, and Rosalind remained on the deck for a while longer, just looking at the scene. She wondered if the Black Horse inn was visible on the shore, or if any of the vessels she could see at anchor belonged to Philip, but then the cool breeze began to make her feel a little cold and she returned to the cabin, where Hetty was sleeping restlessly on the bed, her cheeks still burning with fever.

At last it was time to go ashore, and the captain sent some sailors to carry the luggage to the waiting rowing boat, and to help with Hetty, for the maid was too weak and ill to walk unaided. Rosalind was very worried as the men carried Hetty down the rope ladder to the bobbing boat, then she was climbing down herself, shivering as the stream of cold air swept over her, lifting her hem to reveal her ankles. The boat shoved off and the two men at the oars began to row steadily toward the shore.

As they neared Falmouth, Rosalind saw how very old the town was. The buildings were rambling, with low roofs, and small mullioned windows, and those by the quayside seemed to have their foundations in the water itself. Soon she could hear sounds; the rattle of carts, the ring of iron-toed sea boots upon cobbles, and the clink-clink of pattens, for it had rained heavily the day before and there were many puddles. The customhouse was very busy, with a cluster of small vessels moored alongside, some of them coastal craft, others merely used to ply between the shore and the ships at anchor out on the water.

Sea gulls rose in a screaming cloud from the quay as the rowing boat nudged the foot of some damp, seaweed-strewn stone steps. A nearby fishing vessel had just brought its catch ashore and the gulls were fighting for any scraps. The two sailors made the rowing boat fast and then carried Hetty carefully up the steps. As Rosalind hurried up behind them, she saw them hail an old man with a ponycart, which was led over immediately so that the sick maid could be laid gently inside. The luggage was then quickly carried up from the boat, and when it had been loaded on the cart next to Hetty, the old man asked Rosalind where she wished to be taken.

"To the Black Horse, if you please."

He was a grizzled former sailor, bearded and ruddy, and he gave her a toothless grin. "American, eh?"

"Yes," she replied cautiously, not knowing quite what to expect.

"I sailed out of Americky many a time. 'Tis a grand place."

Relieved, she managed a smile. "Yes, it is."

"Right, then—the Black Horse it is. Daniel Penruthin keeps the finest house in all Falmouth, so you'll be well-looked-after there."

Daniel Penruthin? The landlord who was an old friend of Philip's?

Rosalind sat beside the old man, and the ponycart began to make its way along the quay before turning up into the town.

The streets were narrow and cobbled, and there were many alleys where the buildings seemed to crowd overhead, as if wishing to shut out the sunlight. It was a far cry from the spaciousness and grandeur of Washington. There were English voices all around, mostly with the same accent as the old man's, which she guessed must be Cornish, but occasionally she heard a more refined tone that reminded her of Philip.

She saw a number of soldiers in red coats, as well as blue-uniformed naval officers, and was reminded that Britain was already at war, with Bonaparte's France. There were anti-French placards on some walls, and caricatures of the emperor in a print-shop window, but nowhere did she detect any hostility toward her own nation.

There was congestion at a crossroads, and the ponycart had to halt for a few minutes. She heard a group of men talking on the corner nearby. They were discussing the loss of the *Queen of Falmouth*, for news of the sighting of the longboat had already spread through the town, as always happened when a ship was missing or lost.

The Black Horse was a large hostelry in the very heart of the town, and was obviously an important establishment, judging by the stagecoaches and general bustle in its vicinity. It was a tall building, with a galleried courtyard in the middle, which the ponycart had to wait to enter because a stagecoach was just departing.

Rosalind stared up at the stagecoach in utter amazement, for there were at least eight outside passengers clinging to their seats on the top. There were four inside passengers as well, and the vehicle swayed alarmingly as it negotiated the turn into the steep road that led up out of the town. Several small dogs barked excitedly, dashing after the coach until the coachman's whip flicked in their direction, and they fell back.

The old man urged the ponycart into the crowded yard, where two more stagecoaches were waiting. There was no sunlight because the inn was so tall all around, and Rosalind looked up at the galleries. A maid was hanging sheets out over one of the rails and a waiter was shouting down an order to one of his fellows by the tap-room door. A bell rang as the ticket clerk leaned out of his little wooden office to announce the imminent departure of the Bodmin stage, and the team of the vehicle concerned tossed their heads expectantly as the passengers began to climb on board.

A fine private carriage drove in as the ponycart drew to a standstill in a relatively quiet corner, and a fashionable lady and gentleman alighted, for the Black Horse was considered to be suitable for all walks of life. The old man called to two porters to assist him with Hetty and the luggage, and Rosalind followed them through a low doorway that led into a whitewashed entrance hall with a gleaming red-tiled floor. Hetty was placed on a high-backed settle against the wall, and Rosalind sat with her, watching the lady and gentleman who'd just arrived. They were talking to a tall, white-aproned man whose confident demeanor suggested that in all probability he was Daniel Penruthin.

The trunks and valises were placed beside the settle, and Rosalind gave the old man some coins for his trouble. They were American coins, for she hadn't had time to change them, but he didn't seem to mind, for it was simple enough to go to the customhouse.

When he'd gone, Rosalind looked around again, waiting for the landlord to finish speaking to the lady and gentleman. The entrance hall was long, and a number of doors opened off it, one of them into the dining room, from where an endless stream of waiters passed to and fro. A staircase rose at the far end of the hall, and she could just make out a paneled landing on the floor above. The smell of cooking hung in the warm air, and a fire crackled in the hearth opposite the settle. Next to the fire there were several tables on which stood jugs of clean hot water, bowls, and piles of freshly laundered towels, for the use of guests arriving after long journeys.

A boy who cleaned boots hurried past, and then a barber went quickly to the staircase, followed by his assistant with a bowl of hot water and a razor. Porters struggled in with other people's luggage, and a departing gentleman grumbled under his breath that the place was becoming far too noisy for one to hear one's own thoughts. Rosalind almost had to agree with him, for somewhere on one of the floors above a woman was singing. She had a beautiful trained voice and was going through her scales, but it wasn't long before the sound became tiresome.

It was all quite chaotic, and very alien to one who was used to the peace and quiet of a vast Washington mansion. She suddenly felt very lonely and far away from home, and she quickly took off her glove in order to look at Philip's signet ring. She'd be with him again soon, and then everything would be all right.

The lady and gentleman finished their conversation with the landlord, who called a porter to escort them up to the room that had been reserved for them. Then he turned and approached the settle. He was a big man, with a raw-boned, rosy face and dark eyes. His starched apron crackled as he moved, and his boots squeaked a little. He wore a clean white shirt, a long brown waistcoat, and leather breeches, and his glance went quickly to Hetty's flushed face.

He bowed to Rosalind. "May I be of assistance, madam?"

"I hope so. Are you the landlord?"

"I am, madam. Daniel Penruthin, your servant." He bowed again.

"I'd like rooms, please, for myself and my maid, preferably adjoining. And then I'd like a doctor to attend my maid, for she has a fever."

"Certainly, madam, my son Samuel will go for Dr. Trenance straightaway, and I have the very rooms at the side of the inn, they're not only next to each other, but have a connecting door."

"That sounds excellent. Thank you."

He turned, beckoning to a waiter. "This lady and her maid will be taking the double rooms, so see to it that the fires are made up well."

"Yes, Mr. Penruthin." The waiter hurried away.

The landlord returned his attention to Rosalind. "May I ask how long you will be requiring the rooms?"

"I don't really know. I've just arrived from Washington,

and am on my way to London, but with my maid being ill . . ."

"I quite understand, madam. Be assured that the Black Horse will make you very welcome. Forgive me for asking, but have you just come in on the *Corinth*?"

"Yes."

"Is it true that a longboat from the *Queen of Falmouth* was sighted?"

"Yes, I'm afraid it is."

He lowered his eyes sadly. "We can only hope she hasn't been lost, but we must fear the worst." His glance suddenly fell upon her signet ring, and he looked swiftly at her. "You wouldn't be Miss Carberry, by any chance?"

"Why, yes, but how—"

"That's Lord Southvale's ring, madam. I'd know it anywhere. I have the honor to be a good acquaintance of his, and he stayed here when he returned from Washington a month or so back. He dined privately with my wife and me, as always he does, and he told us all about you, Miss Carberry. Oh, he was a different man from the one who'd sailed from here back in the early summer, much happier by far, and it made us so glad to see him so improved. It was all on account of you, Miss Carberry; he made that plain enough."

She flushed with sudden pleasure, and her sense of isolation began to fade a little. "Thank you for saying so, Mr. Penruthin."

"Not at all, Miss Carberry. Now you're doubly welcome at the Black Horse; indeed, there could be few persons more welcome here than the future Lady Southvale."

"Thank you," she said again.

The singing from somewhere above became suddenly louder than ever, as the unseen woman broke into a full-throated aria, ending on a heart-stopping high note that Rosalind was sure would shatter every windowpane in the building.

The landlord raised his eyes heavenward. "That's Signora

Segati, an opera singer from La Scala in Milan. She's resting here after her voyage from Italy and will soon go to London to sing at the Italian Opera House.''

He made it sound as if it wouldn't be soon enough as far as he was concerned. Rosalind smiled a little. ''She has a very, er, powerful voice.''

''She has indeed. We've been having Mr. Mozart with our breakfast, Mr. Handel with our luncheon, and Mr. Purcell with our dinner for nearly a week now, but I understand it's only to go on for a day or so more. Speaking of meals, have you eaten this morning?''

''No, I haven't.''

''I'll see to it that a good breakfast is served in your room, Miss Carberry, for I doubt if you'll wish to eat in our very crowded dining room, not after just coming ashore, anyway.''

''I'd prefer to eat in my room, yes.''

''I'll take you up there right now, and carry your maid myself, then I'll see to it that Samuel goes immediately for Dr. Trenance.''

He turned to Hetty, lifting her as if she weighed nothing at all, and as Rosalind followed him up the staircase, Hetty's illness was suddenly the only blot on her horizon, for she was confident she'd done the right thing in coming here to England.

But as she was going to learn to her cost, this new confidence was very misplaced.

8

The two adjoining rooms were plainly but comfortably furnished. They were on the first floor, their narrow mullioned windows overlooking a dark alley at the side of the inn, so that there wasn't a great deal of sunlight penetrating the panes. Their walls were paneled in dark oak, and faded blue velvet hung at the windows and on the four-poster bed in the larger room. Well-worn rugs were scattered on the polished wooden floors, and fires crackled pleasantly in the hearths, the flame light flickering over everything. There was a scent of herbs from several little posies that had been pinned beneath the mantelpieces. It was a pleasant scent, fresh and clean.

Mr. Penruthin laid Hetty carefully on the bed in the smaller room and then hurried away to send for the doctor and to have breakfast brought up for Rosalind. Some porters brought the luggage in, setting it on the floor in Rosalind's room, and she quickly unpacked the maid's nightgown, going to take Hetty's blue chemise gown off again and make her as comfortable as possible in her night things. She managed to get the maid into the bed, tucking her in carefully, and then looked anxiously at her, hoping that the doctor would be able to help. Oh, please, don't let anything happen to Hetty.

Removing her own cloak, Rosalind tossed it over a chair and then went to the window, looking down into the alley below. Signora Segati was in a nearby room, and her singing was very loud. Two seamen walked along the alley, their boots ringing, and they glanced up in astonishment as they heard the trilling, but then their attention was drawn away by a pretty milkmaid hurrying past in the opposite direction, her empty pails swinging on her yoke. They whistled and called after her, but she kept her nose in the air and ignored them with as much hauteur as a fine lady. Rosalind smiled a little, for it was a scene that could have taken place anywhere in the world, not just here in Falmouth. Men would always ogle a pretty girl, and pretty girls would always show their scorn, and their hidden pleasure, by being haughty and dismissive.

One of the inn's maids brought a tray set with a rather hearty breakfast, and Rosalind sat by the fire attempting to do justice to the eggs, bacon, sausages, and tomatoes, the fresh bread rolls, and the pot of good tea. It had been over three weeks since she'd eaten such fine food, but although she knew she should eat properly, she was too worried about Hetty to have a hearty appetite.

Dr. Trenance came shortly afterward and swiftly declared that the maid was suffering from a putrid sea fever that would have to run its course. He prescribed warmth and plenty of rest, constant nursing, as much fluid as the patient could be persuaded to drink, and the judicious application of laudanum. He didn't think the fever was contagious, but had been brought on by the maid's own foolishness, and he didn't think she would be well enough to continue the journey to London for at least two weeks.

Rosalind was relieved that Hetty would recover, but dismayed at the thought of such a long wait. The doctor administered the first dose of laudanum, and then left, saying that he would return the next day. When he'd gone, Mr. Penruthin came to see Rosalind, advising her to sleep if she could and inviting her to dine with his family that evening.

The thought of sleep was very tempting, for it hadn't been possible to do so properly during the voyage, and so Rosalind accepted his invitation and then drew the curtains of her room. Hetty was already asleep, the laudanum had seen to that, and when Signora Segati's singing ceased at last, Rosalind sank thankfully into a deep, restorative sleep.

She must have needed the rest more than she'd realized, for it was dark when she was aroused by an inn maid who'd crept in to tend the fires.

Rosalind got up quickly and went to see how Hetty was. The maid was still asleep, her cheeks flushed, but she woke up sufficiently to take a long drink of water. Lighting the candles in her room, Rosalind then selected a gown from her luggage, a pale-green dimity that she knew traveled well and wouldn't look too crumpled for dining with the Penruthins.

She was just endeavoring to pin her hair up again when there was a knock at her door. "Yes?" She turned from the dressing-table mirror, still pinning a curl into place.

A tall young man entered. He bore a striking resemblance to the landlord, and she guessed immediately that he was Samuel, the Penruthins' son. He wore a gray coat and leather breeches, and he bowed a little awkwardly.

"Begging your pardon, Miss Carberry, but I've been sent to tell you dinner will be served in half an hour's time."

"Thank you."

"A maid will come to conduct you."

"Thank you."

He bowed again, his glance moving fleetingly toward the adjoining door into Hetty's room, then he withdrew.

As the door closed behind him, Rosalind heard a heavily accented female voice addressing him. "Ah, Signor Penrutti, I vish to speak with you."

Samuel had halted. "Can I be of assistance, *signora*?"

"I vish to leave for London the day after tomorrow, and so I vish you to secure me a good post chaise, for a stagecoach vill not do at all."

"Very well, *signora*. I'll attend to your request."

"Excellent."

Then there was silence again, Signora Segati evidently having returned to her room and Samuel to whatever he had to do.

Rosalind looked in the mirror again, raising her aching arms to finish combing and pinning her hair. Oh, how difficult it was to achieve an adequate coiffure without Hetty's capable assistance.

An inn maid came to conduct her to dinner. "If you'll come this way, madam," she said, bobbing a curtsy.

Rosalind followed her from the room and down the staircase. The inn was no less noisy, now that it was dark. There were still stagecoaches coming and going in the yard, and the dining room sounded as if it was filled to capacity. As she and Samuel reached the foot of the stairs, a waiter emerged from the room, pausing to wedge the door open. She looked past him and saw a great assortment of people seated around the large circular tables. There were ladies and gentlemen, clergymen, naval officers, well-to-do farmers and their families, and a large group of red-uniformed army officers.

Then Samuel led her through another door and along a narrow passage into the kitchens, which were, if possible, even more a hive of industry and noise than the dining room. The stone-flagged floor was spotlessly clean, and there was an immense fireplace, blackened with the smoke of ages, where a number of huge copper kettles were kept constantly at the boil. There were metal trivets standing before the heat, and on them were pans of varying size, some sizzling, some steaming, and some boiling with thick sauces. A huge joint of beef was being turned on a spit by a small boy whose face was red from the heat and exertion, a cook was drawing a fresh batch of bread from a wall oven, and a small army of maids and kitchen boys was chopping and peeling vegetables at several well-scrubbed tables. A fat man was preparing meat on a marble slab at the far end of the room, and a woman was pumping water at a stone sink by a window. Cold viands, strings of onions and drying mushrooms, and apples were suspended from the beamed ceiling, and a maid was climbing up a ladder to lift down a large bunch of dried herbs from another hook close to the fireplace.

Rosalind was conscious of interested glances upon her as she followed the maid through toward the Penruthins' private rooms at the rear, and she knew that everyone at the inn was now aware that she was the future Lady Southvale.

Mr. and Mrs. Penruthin, but not their son, were waiting in a cozy parlor where the chairs were covered with green-and-white chintz. The floor was stone-flagged, like the kitchens, and the walls had been recently whitewashed. A splendid collection of brass candlesticks stood on the high mantelpiece, and a white-clothed table had been laid with the very best crockery and cutlery the inn could offer.

The landlord's wife was a round, cheerful countrywoman, and looked very neat and precise in a gray-and-white-checkered gown, starched white apron, and large, frilled mobcap. Her brown hair was plaited and coiled at the back of her head, and she had long-lashed brown eyes that reminded Rosalind of a King Charles spaniel.

The Penruthins were determined both to make her feel welcome and to serve her with a delicious meal, and they succeeded. The dinner commenced with a light and tasty clear onion soup, followed by a brace of roast partridge, stuffed with mushrooms; the partridges were accompanied by vegetables so fresh that they must have been pulled from the earth only minutes before being cooked. As a dessert there were raspberries preserved in honey, served with the clotted cream for which Cornwall was so famous. After the somewhat dismal meals on board the *Corinth*, Rosalind found it almost too appetizing for words.

Conversation was wide-ranging, covering topics as varied as the state of the war in Spain, Bonaparte's qualities as a general, the Prince Regent's lavish hospitality at Carlton House, and whether mad King George would ever recover.

Everyone tactfully steered clear of whether there would be war between Britain and America, but clearly it was at the back of all their minds—Rosalind's for obvious reasons, and the Penruthins' because Falmouth had such strong connections with the former colony across the Atlantic.

Philip was also mentioned, and Rosalind was conscious of her hosts' great liking and respect for him. He was spoken of as a shining example of all that was admirable in the aristrocracy, and they made it plain that they were glad he was to marry again. From time to time Rosalind felt Mrs. Penruthin's gaze upon her in an oddly speculative way, and never more so than when she, Rosalind, mentioned in passing that she hoped she could adequately replace the first Lady Southvale.

They'd almost finished when Samuel came to tell his father that a gentleman in the dining room was refusing to pay his bill. Mr. Penruthin quickly excused himself from the table and hurried away with his son.

In the ensuing silence, Mrs. Penruthin studied Rosalind for a long moment before speaking, and when she did, she chose her words very carefully. "I know I have no right to ask, Miss Carberry, but are you truly apprehensive about following in the first Lady Southvale's footsteps?"

It was an unexpectedly direct question, but Rosalind chose to answer it all the same. "Yes, Mrs. Penruthin, I believe I am," she admitted, remembering how glowingly Philip had described his first wife.

"Then don't be, for she was undoubtedly the most spiteful, selfish, disagreeable cat in all the world, and I, for one, wasn't at all sad when she was lost in that shipwreck. Good riddance to her, that's what I said at the time, and it's still what I say now. She was a bad lot, and I believe her husband was one of the few people never to have realized the fact."

9

Rosalind stared at her, thoroughly amazed by such frankness.

Mrs. Penruthin smiled a little. "Have I shocked you, my dear?"

"Just a little."

"Forgive me, but I felt you should know what she was really like. It's my guess that when you think of her, you imagine a beautiful, delightful creature whose tragic death broke her adoring husband's heart and whose loss was mourned by all who knew her. Am I right?"

Rosalind hesitated, not really wanting to indulge in such a conversation, but curious to know more. She nodded slowly. "Yes, I suppose that's more or less how I think of her."

"I thought so. Well, she *was* beautiful, that much is true, and she was all sweetness and light when Lord Southvale was near, but when she was on her own, it was a different matter. She stayed here often when she was going to visit her family in Ireland, and we saw both sides of her." Mrs. Penruthin paused. "Nothing pleased her when she stayed here on her own, and she thought little of demanding someone's dismissal if things didn't go as she wished. The last time she was here on her own, Mr. Penruthin wouldn't bow to her wishes when she wanted a stableboy punished for not having her horse saddled in readiness for her morning ride on the moor. It had been raining heavily the night before, and she'd said she wouldn't need the horse, but when she woke up the next day, the sun was out, and it was her contention that the stableboy should have known she'd need the horse, after all. It was unreasonable, and Mr. Penruthin stood up to her, so much so that he said he'd appeal direct to Lord Southvale if she persisted. She showed her deep displeasure by removing immediately to the Crown and Anchor, and she stayed there as well on her return from the trip to Ireland. We expected her to blacken us with Lord Southvale, but all she apparently said to him was that she preferred to stay at the Crown and Anchor because it was right by the harbor, and therefore more convenient. She obviously didn't want to risk his lordship believing our version of events.''

Rosalind didn't know what to say, for it was hardly a flattering picture of Philip's first wife.

Mrs. Penruthin sighed. ''Oh, she was a clever liar, and a fine actress, and Lord Southvale never knew her for what she really was. All she cared about was getting her own way no matter what, and she didn't worry who she hurt in the process. But she had to be careful where her husband was concerned, for although he doted on her and gave her everything she wanted, all that would have come to an end if he'd realized the truth about her. She didn't love him, I'm sure, but she liked having all such a man could give her, and so to him she was always an angel, while to the rest of us she was the devil incarnate.''

''I can't believe she was really so bad,'' said Rosalind, quite bemused by what she'd been told.

''To my mind she was less than perfect in other ways too, but I couldn't prove it.''

''What do you mean?''

The Cornishwoman hesitated to say anything else, but then went on. ''That last time she stayed in Falmouth, at the Crown and Anchor, there was a foreign gentleman staying here with us. They were seen riding together on the moor.''

Rosalind stared at her. ''Are you suggesting . . . ?''

''As I said, I couldn't prove anything, but I saw how they were when they were together.''

''Who was he?''

''A Portuguese nobleman by the name of Dom Rodrigo de Freire. He'd been in England for some three months, visiting London after serving with the Duke of Wellington in Spain. He was very handsome and dashing, and very wealthy, for he had fine estates outside Lisbon. His ship set sail for Portugal on the same tide that hers left for Ireland.''

''Mrs. Penruthin, you surely can't be saying that simply because they were occasionally seen riding together on the moor . . .''

''Every day, Miss Carberry, they rode together every day. She'd ride up past us, and he'd leave about ten minutes later. She'd wait for him up by the crossroads and then they'd ride off together. They didn't come back until several hours later. I simply can't believe that it was all innocent, but maybe I'm too cynical after all the goings-on I've seen in this inn over the years. A landlord's wife develops a sixth sense about such things, you know, but whether or not she and Dom Rodrigo were more to each other than they should have been, nothing alters the fact that she wasn't the sweet creature Lord Southvale thought she was, and therefore not the sort of woman you have any need to go in awe of.''

Rosalind rose slowly to her feet and went to a window. She held a curtain aside to look out and found herself gazing at the courtyard. A sea mist had risen, and although the yard was still bustling, everything was indistinct, as if seen through a veil. The glow of lamps and lanterns was diffused and sounds seemed to be muffled. ''Why did you tell me all this, Mrs. Penruthin?'' she asked without glancing back into the parlor.

''Because I'm a second wife, too, my dear. There was another Mrs. Penruthin before me, and I had to battle against her memory. She seemed to have been a paragon of all the virtues, and I was constantly striving to live up to her example. Then, one wonderful day, I found out by chance that she'd had a fault, after all—two faults, to be precise: twin daughters born out of wedlock before she'd even met Mr. Penruthin. She hadn't said a word about them and behaved as if she was untarnished, giving herself airs and graces, and actually having the neck to look down on others who'd fallen by the same wayside as she herself. Feet of clay she had, Miss Carberry, just like Lady Southvale. I didn't tell Mr. Penruthin the truth about her, for I didn't want to hurt him, but I felt so much better once I'd discovered her flaws. I could be myself after that, and I know I've made him much happier than she ever did. You'll make Lord Southvale happier as well, my dear, for you really do have all the qualities he thought she had. You're the best thing that could have happened to him, I knew that when I saw how changed he was on his return from Washington. He's yours now, Miss Carberry, so just you get on with your life and don't give that wicked first wife of his any thought at all.'' The landlord's wife got up from her seat and came to stand by Rosalind, putting a reassuring hand briefly on her arm. "I wish you every good fortune in your marriage, my dear, for in Lord Southvale you have a man second to none, and I sincerely hope that one day you and he will visit the Black Horse, so that we can show you both how much we welcome you.''

Rosalind smiled at her. "Thank you, Mrs. Penruthin.''

"As to what I so indiscreetly said about her ladyship and Dom Rodrigo . . .''

"Yes?''

"I'd be grateful if you forgot I ever said it, for I had no right. I don't know the truth about them, and I could be wrong. I'm not wrong about what a spiteful, unpleasant creature she was, though, and I don't take back another word.''

Later that same night, when Rosalind had retired to her

bed in Falmouth, Philip sat alone in the library at Greys,
his fine country house some five miles north of London, overlooking Hampstead Heath. It was a magnificent mansion,
built in the classical style by Robert Adam, with two
symmetrical single-story wings projecting on either side.
Porticoed, with a decorative pediment supported on four
fluted Corinthian columns, Greys was visible for many miles
over the heath. It stood on a lofty grassy terrace, facing south
over a small valley containing an ornamental lake, and it was
set in a splendid park that had been laid out some twenty
years before by Humphrey Repton.

Hampstead Heath stretched away on all sides, but nowhere
was it higher than the house, which consequently enjoyed
an enviable veiw over London, visibility on a clear day
reaching as far as the dome of St. Paul's cathedral. But it
was dark now, and the moon was obscured by clouds, so
nothing could be seen outside the only library window that
was unshuttered.

The library at Greys was housed in one of the single-story
wings, the other contained a conservatory of rare and exotic
plants. Dust sheets covered the furniture, and all the windows
were shuttered and curtained, for the house was closed. The
only people who knew Lord Southvale was there were the
permanent staff, especially the housekeeper, Mrs. Simmons.

He sat wearily at the ornate writing desk his father had
acquired in Rome during his grand tour. A lighted, four-
branched candlestick was before him, the soft glow falling
over a silver-gilt inkstand, and the untouched sheet of vellum
that lay in readiness for the letter he wished with all his heart
he didn't have to compose.

His black hair was disheveled, and his blue eyes tired. He
wore an indigo coat, white cord breeches, and a grey-and-
white-striped marcella waistcoat that he hadn't bothered to
button. His frilled shirt was undone at the throat, and his
crumpled neckcloth hung loose. He hadn't been sleeping
because of all that was on his mind, and it showed in his
pallor and the shadows beneath his eyes. The candles

illuminated only the desk, and all around him, the library was in shadow. He stared unhappily at the sheet of vellum. This letter was the very last he'd ever wished to write, but he had no choice in the matter. He glanced at the glass and half-empty decanter of cognac he'd placed nearby, then he got up to pour himself some more, for it helped to dull the pain he felt inside.

Swirling the liberally filled glass, he went to unshutter a window and look out. He could just see the lights of London in the distance, but a mist was rising, rolling from the sea as the temperature of the autumn night slipped below freezing. His breath touched the glass, and he turned away with a shiver, crossing to the fireplace to toss another log on the dying fire. As he pressed it firmly down with his boot, a cloud of brilliant sparks fled up the chimney, and new flames began to lick around the dry wood.

Shadows leapt over the library, and his glance was drawn inexorably to a framed pencil sketch on the wall nearby. It was the preliminary drawing for a full-length portrait of his first wife, with a view of Greys itself in the background. The finished portrait now hung in the drawing room at Southvale House, his London residence overlooking Green Park, but he'd liked the pencil sketch so much that he'd had it framed.

He gazed at the lovely figure, and especially at the face, so magically beautiful that it hurt even now to look at it. Celia, with her lustrous dark curls, flawless skin, heart-shaped face, and incomparable lilac eyes. The gown she'd worn for the portrait had been made of delicate pink satin, and the artist, having a great admiration for Mr. Gainsborough, had placed his subject against a leaden, thundery sky. It was a dramatic portrait, vivid and lifelike in the finished article, ethereal and dreamlike in this preliminary pencil sketch.

He raised his glass. "Oh, Celia, how could I have forgotten you?" he murmured, draining the glass and grimacing as the fiery liquid burned his throat.

The clock on the mantelpiece began to strike midnight, and he turned away from the sketch. Midnight. The witching hour. He thought of the Fourth of July ball in Washington and the moment when he'd seen Rosalind in her ice-green silk gown. It had been just after midnight when he'd danced that minuet with her. Oh, the witching hour indeed . . . Sweet, innocent Rosalind.

He looked at the writing desk again and the sheet of vellum that he had to apply himself to. He'd already sent a brief note, so brief that it had almost been terse, and now a fuller explanation was due. He wished the cognac had had more effect, but it hardly seemed to have touched him tonight.

With a heavy heart he returned to his chair, putting down the glass and taking up his pen. He did no one any favors by putting off the inevitable. Fate had dealt him a bitter hand, and he had no option but to play it.

10

The mist lifted at dawn in Falmouth, and by the time Dr. Trenance came to see Hetty again, the sun was shining on another fine autumn day.

Rosalind waited by the window as he examined the maid. She wore the same apricot wool gown she'd had on to disembark from the *Corinth*, and her golden hair was simply brushed loose about her shoulders. Some children were playing in the alley below the window, and Signora Segati was again singing her interminable scales. A fresh fire crackled in the hearth, and another stagecoach rattled out of the yard, its horn wavering as it proceeded up the steep hill out of the town.

Drawing her white wool shawl more closely around her shoulders, Rosalind turned to watch the doctor as he examined Hetty. The maid seemed much better this morning, encouraging the hope that she'd recover before the two weeks he'd predicted the day before.

Dr. Trenance straightened. He was a thin, foxy-faced man with a pointed nose, and the black he wore made him seem thinner than ever. He came to Rosalind. "There is very slight improvement," he said in a qualified tone.

"More than slight, surely?"

"I'm afraid that the laudanum masks a great deal."

Her lips parted anxiously. "Are you telling me that she's . . . ?"

"A little worse than I anticipated? Yes, I fear so. She will recover, have no fear of that, for it isn't a fatal fever, but it will take longer for her to recuperate than I at first believed. There is a weakness there, a quivering of the pulse, and the malaise appears to have taken much more of a toll of her reserves than was apparent yesterday." He glanced at the maid, who appeared to be asleep again.

Rosalind looked at him in dismay. "Is there anything else we can do to aid her recovery?"

"We can only wait, madam."

"So, she won't be able to travel to London in two weeks?"

"Indeed, no. I would not wish her to undertake a journey like that for at least a month, and even then it would not be wise for her to resume her duties."

"I see." Rosalind was disheartened, for there always seemed to be something to force her to again postpone her plans. First it had been two weeks before they could leave Falmouth, now it was a month or more.

The doctor went to pick up his bag. "I hope to be able to cease the administering of laudanum in about a week's time, and after that, I will prescribe Mrs. Penruthin's lavender infusion, which I have always found to be a sovereign remedy for such debilitating fevers. I will call again in two days' time. Good day to you, Miss Carberry."

"Good day, Dr. Trenance."

As the door closed behind him, she turned to look out of the window again. Perhaps she should write to Philip and explain where she was. He could then come to her, and at least they'd see each other before another month was out.

There was another tap at the door, and Mrs. Penruthin came in. "I'm so sorry your maid isn't as well as we'd hoped, my dear."

"So am I," replied Rosalind. "But at least she's going to get better."

"Do you wish to stay here until then?"

"I have to."

"A month is a long time."

"I know." Rosalind closed her eyes as Signora Segati soared to a particularly high note.

Mrs. Penruthin came closer. "My dear, you don't have to stay here, for we'll gladly take care of your maid."

Rosalind turned. "Oh, I couldn't possibly consider—"

"You've come all this way to be with Lord Southvale, my dear, not to languish in Falmouth because your maid is ill. We hold his lordship in very high regard, and if we can be of any assistance, then we're more than happy to help. Signora Segati has hired a post chaise to leave for London tomorrow morning, and only she and her maid will occupy the carriage. I know that she would welcome the company of another lady, and if you wish me to approach her on your behalf . . ."

Rosalind was tempted, but shook her head, for her conscience wouldn't allow her to desert Hetty, not even if she'd be with people as kind and considerate as the Penruthins. "I'd prefer to stay."

The Cornishwoman smiled understandingly. "Well, if you change your mind, you have only to tell me. It could all be arranged in a few moments, and you could be with his lordship again in days, rather than weeks. Just you think about it."

As the landlord's wife withdrew, Hetty spoke weakly from the bed. "Please go without me, madam."

Rosalind turned a little guiltily. "I thought you were asleep."

"I heard everything. She's right, you should go with the *signora*."

"And leave you on your own?"

"I'll be all right. Miss Carberry, I'll feel very bad if you stay just because of me."

"Oh, Hetty . . ."

"Please tell her you'll go with the *signora*, Miss Carberry, and when I'm better, I'll follow you to London." The maid's eyes were lackluster, but the earnestness she felt could still be made out in them. "Please, Miss Carberry."

Rosalind hesitated.

Hetty pressed her again. "I'll get better more quickly if I know I haven't stopped you from being with Lord Southvale."

Rosalind smiled. "Very well, Hetty, I'll go, provided, that is, that the *signora* will agree."

The *signora* was delighted at the prospect of someone to converse with during the journey, and gladly consented when Mrs. Penruthin put the matter to her. That night the two prospective travel companions dined together in the crowded inn dining room, and Rosalind emerged from the experience knowing that the following few days were going to be anything but restful. The *signora* was a very voluble, plump, olive-skinned woman with shining black eyes and black hair that she wore in a rather too youthful tumble of ringlets. She liked to wear rouge and had a predilection for lace, flounces of which sprang from the ample bodices of her gowns. She also liked wide-brimmed hats sporting waving plumes, items of apparel that didn't bode well for a journey in the confines of a post chaise. The *signora*'s favorite topic of conversation was herself, and Rosalind knew that by the time they reached the capital, every detail of the singer's life would have been related time and time again.

The chaise was set to leave just after first light the next morning, and it arrived promptly in the yard.

The luggage of both Rosalind and the *signora* was carefully loaded in the boot, and as the boot was closed, the two women emerged from the inn, followed by the signora's maid. Rosalind wore her fur-trimmed cloak over the apricot wool gown, and there was a straw bonnet on her head. Her hair was pinned up in a plain knot, with a soft edging of curls framing her face. It had taken her a long time to achieve the style, but at least she didn't look untidy next to Signora Segati.

Rosalind settled back in her seat and barely had time to wave farewell to the Penruthins before the chaise lurched forward on the start of its two-hundred-and-fifty-mile journey east to London. The horses' hooves struck sparks from the cobbled street as the postboys urged them up the hill out of the town. As the buildings on the outskirts of Falmouth faded swiftly away behind, Rosalind looked out to see the anchorage of Carrick Roads shining in the sunshine below. The ships looked like toys, far too fragile for the rigors of the open sea, and she tried to make out the *Corinth*, but the chaise swept over the brow of the moor before she could.

The air was fresh and sweet, a mixture of heather, gorse, and moorland grass, and there were sheep and goats nibbling at the tips of the gorse. Sea gulls soared white against the blue sky, and somewhere beyond the rattle of the chaise she could hear the lonely cry of a curlew. But already the *signora* was talking, her heavily accented voice commencing the history of her Milanese family.

In spite of the *signora's* endless chattering, it was still possible to enjoy the journey, for there was so much to see. England was very different from America, and seemed very small and intimate after the wide open spaces she'd always known. The towns and villages were very old, with idyllic thatched cottages, fine medieval churches, rambling inns, and ancient market squares, some of which had been in use since before the Norman Conquest. Centuries-old farms nestled on hilltops, and watermills straddled racing streams. Windmills caught the breeze, orchards were heavy with fruit, and fine mansions presided over noble parks; there was prosperity all around, and little evidence at all of the war against France that had been in progress for so long now.

By the morning of the last day of the journey, Rosalind was beginning to wilt under the endless sound of the *signora's* voice, but took comfort in the knowledge that it would all be over in a matter of hours now. They'd stayed overnight at an inn in Newbury, and she chose her clothes very carefully for the final part of the journey, because at the end of it, she'd see Philip again and she wanted to look her very best.

She put on a primrose sprigged muslin and matching pelisse, and a wide-brimmed primrose muslin hat tied on with green satin ribbons the same color as her eyes. She struggled again with her hair, combing and pinning laboriously until she'd achieved the style she wanted, a loose knot at the back of her head, with a single heavy ringlet tumbling from it.

The chaise set off for the last time, and it wasn't long before the close proximity of the capital became evident. By midday there was much more traffic on the road, fewer country wagons and carts, but many more private carriages drawn by blood horses. Stagecoaches drove swiftly to and from the capital, outpaced by the occasional mail coach, and both were easily outstripped by the light phaetons, curricles, and gigs driven by dashing young gentlemen dressed in the very tippy of high fashion.

The towns were closer together now, and more prosperous than ever. Fine villas lined the highway, and gentlemen's residences were set in neat grounds, agreeable without being too grand. There were still elegant mansions and great parks, and Rosalind was reminded that Philip's country seat, Greys, was only five miles outside the capital.

Shadows were lengthening as the chaise drove across Hounslow Heath, once the haunt of highwaymen, and then they were on the last turnpike into the city. Spires and domes appeared on the eastern horizon ahead as the short autumn afternoon drew to a close, and the final slanting rays of the sun fell across St. Paul's itself, making it gleam like a beacon.

There was little left of the sun, except a blaze of crimson in the west, as the postboys urged their tired horses past the royal palace of Kensington, turning briefly off the main highway to leave the *signora* and her maid at an address in Knightsbridge. Her luggage was unloaded, and then Rosalind waved good-bye to her as the now quiet chaise drove on toward St. James's.

Hyde Park loomed on the left, leafy, spacious acres that

in daytime saw the parade of fashionable society along Rotten Row. St. George's Hospital, its windows dimly lit, swept by on the right, and then she saw the grand facade of Apsley House, standing on the corner of Park Lane and Piccadilly. Daylight had gone completely now, and the chaise lamps were lit, as were the lamps of all other vehicles on the crowded city roads. Shop windows were illuminated, and streetlamps kindled, so that all was light and bright in Piccadilly, the thoroughfare that took the chaise eastward toward exclusive St. James's.

Piccadilly was one of the noisiest and most exciting streets that Rosalind had ever seen. The southern boundary was taken up with the wall and trees of Green Park, but the northern side was a long line of shops, inns, stagecoach ticket offices, clubs, lodging houses, and impressive private residences. Wonderful displays of goods were shown off in shop windows, to be gazed at by the elegant ladies and gentlemen who strolled with leisurely ease in the early evening.

Just before the junction with Bond Street, the chaise turned south into St. James's Street, at the end of which stood St. James's Palace itself. It was a gentlemen's street, containing all the most superior clubs, from White's and Boodle's, to Brooks' and the Thatched House. In nearby King Street she knew she would find Almack's, that most select temple of high fashion, from which it was a disaster to be excluded.

But the close proximity of Almack's meant little to her as she toyed nervously with Philip's signet ring through her glove. She was only a minute or so away from her destination now, and her pulse had quickened in anticipation. Oh, how she longed to see him again, to be in his arms with his lips over hers.

The chaise turned again, this time westward into St. James's Place, at the end of which stood Southvale House. By the light of the streetlamps she could see superb town houses on either side, while directly ahead it was just possible to make out the autumn foliage of the trees in Green Park.

Tall wrought-iron gates loomed on the left, at the very end of what proved to be a cul-de-sac, and as the chaise drove through them into the courtyard, she looked up to see stone griffins standing fiercely on the tops of the post.

Southvale House itself was larger and more magnificent than any other building in the street. Its roofline was marked by a stone balustrade on top of which were placed statues of gods and griffins, and the two upper stories boasted handsome pediments supported on Doric columns. A double flight of steps led up to the door, which opened immediately the chaise was perceived in the courtyard.

A rather superior butler emerged, dressed very grandly in a brown coat with velvet lapels, beige knee breeches, and a powdered wig. He was accompanied by two footmen in fawn-and-gold livery, who positioned themselves very precisely on either side of the door while the butler descended the steps. One of the postboys had dismounted and came to open the chaise door for Rosalind, but as she alighted, the butler spoke to her. "I think you may have called at the wrong address, madam. This is Southvale House."

"I'm well aware that this is Southvale House," she replied a little coolly, disliking his manner. "It's upon Lord Southvale that I'm calling."

"His lordship is not at home."

Not at home? Her heart sank, for that hadn't been a possibility she'd even thought about. "Then perhaps Lady Eleanor is at home? Or Miss de Grey?"

"No, madam, they both have a dinner engagement this evening."

"When do you expect someone to be at home?"

"I really cannot say, madam," he replied evasively, for she was a complete stranger. "Perhaps if you call again tomorrow . . ."

"I haven't come all this way simply to call again tomorrow," she replied shortly, disliking his manner more and more. "My name is Miss Carberry."

"Madam?" He looked blankly at her, the name evidently meaning nothing to him.

"Hasn't Lord Southvale mentioned me?" she asked, an uneasy finger touching her heart.

"No, madam, I fear he has not."

She stared at him, totally taken by surprise. But why hadn't Philip said anything about her? What on earth reason could there be for such a glaring omission?

The butler was eager to be rid of a caller he felt had no legitimate business at the house. "As I said, madam, perhaps if you call again tomorrow . . ."

"Does this mean anything to you?" she asked, taking off her glove and holding up her left hand.

He recognized the ring immediately, and his lips parted in astonishment. "It—it's Lord Southvale's signet ring, madam."

"And does the finger I'm wearing it on suggest anything to you?" she inquired, her tone frosty because she was suddenly so uneasy.

He swallowed. "Well, yes, madam, but—"

"No buts, sir, for it's no accident that the ring is on the fourth finger of my left hand. While he was in America, Lord Southvale did me the honor of asking me to be his wife, and I accepted. I've traveled all the way here from my home in Washington, and I have no intention whatsoever of calling again tomorrow. I rather think his lordship will be most displeased with you when he hears how dismally you've treated me."

The two footmen by the doorway had heard everything and exchanged astonished, openmouthed glances.

The butler gaped at her, his composure completely rattled. "Madam, I know nothing at all about you. Lord Southvale hasn't said anything about marrying again."

It was a point that was of no small concern to Rosalind herself, although she was determined not to let the butler realize it. "I'm sure he has his reasons, sir, but in the meantime I expect to be offered the hospitality of this house. When is Lord Southvale expected to return?''

"I don't know, madam. Indeed, no one here knows where he's been for several weeks now.''

"Several *weeks*?''

"Yes, madam. He left without saying where he would be or when he'd be back, although we do know that he has a very important appointment at the Foreign Office in a week's time.''

Her heart sank still further. Was it to be another long week before she saw him? She drew a slow breath. "But Lady Eleanor and Miss de Grey will be here later this evening?''

"Yes, madam.''

"Then I'll wait inside for them.''

He didn't know what to do, and the quandary was evident on his face. He didn't know anything about her, but she was wearing his master's signet ring, and if her story was true, by doing the wrong thing now he'd fall foul of the next Lady Southvale. Discretion was the greater part of valor, and he gave her a gracious bow. "Under the circumstances, Miss Carberry, I feel I must indeed offer you the hospitality of Southvale House.'' He turned, beckoning to the two footmen, ordering the first one to commence unloading her luggage from the chaise. The second one he drew a little to one side, speaking in an undertone that she wasn't intended to hear, but that carried quite clearly. "Go and find Mr. Beaufort without delay. Tell him he's needed here very urgently.''

"Will he be at his address in Piccadilly, Mr. Richardson?''

The butler looked witheringly at him. "On the Marquess of Aldington's first night in town after coming into his inheritance? Don't be foolish, man," he snapped. "He'll be at one of his clubs, White's probably, attempting to relieve the marquess of as much of his fortune as humanly possible.''

The footman was openly appalled. "Call him away from his club, Mr. Richardson? He won't like it.''

"This is much more important than his need to settle his

gambling debts. Find him and tell him he must come here straightaway.''

''Yes, Mr. Richardson.'' Looking less than enthusiastic about his task, the unfortunate footman ran away across the courtyard, vanishing between the gates into St. James's Place.

Rosalind watched him, wondering who this Mr. Beaufort was. Obviously he was a relative of Celia's, but Philip had never mentioned his first wife's family. Maybe he was Celia's father, or her uncle; whoever he was, he evidently wasn't amenable to being disturbed from the gaming tables.

The butler was addressing her. ''If you will come this way, madam.''

She roused herself from her thoughts, following him up the steps to the door of the house. She felt very unsettled and anxious, for this wasn't the welcome she'd been expecting. Why hadn't Philip said anything about her? A chill seemed to have settled over her. Something was very wrong, and she couldn't even begin to guess what it might be.

11

The entrance hall was decorated and furnished in the Chinese style, and the blend of soft blues, greens, pinks, and, above all, gold was so exquisitely beautiful that it made Rosalind's breath catch in wonder.

Exotic gilded lanterns were suspended from a lofty domed ceiling just beneath the attic story, and the marble-balustraded floors in between encircled the area in galleries supported on Ionic columns. These floors were approached up a handsome staircase made of pink marble, with banisters fashioned like slender golden dragons. The walls were hung with ice-blue silk that had been painted in a beautiful design of lotus blossoms and peacocks, and the floor was tiled in a pattern of leaves and fish, for all the world like a pool in an Oriental garden.

Flames licked gently around glowing coals in the ornate black marble fireplace to one side, and there were several elegant blue velvet sofas, their arms and legs inlaid with ivory and mother-of-pearl. In the center of the floor stood a circular table with a top made of engraved silver. All the doors that opened off the ground floor, and the floors above, had gilded architraves of particular richness, and each door was guarded on either side by lifesize porcelain figures of mandarins, holding aloft lighted lamps that, together with the lanterns hanging from the ceiling, made everything almost dazzlingly bright after the darkness outside.

The butler led her to the staircase, and as they began to ascend, the footman carried in the first item of her luggage, setting it carefully on the floor. Double doors faced the top of the first rise of the staircase, and these the butler flung open to reveal a dimly lit green-and-gold drawing room.

Like the rest of the house so far, it was opulently decorated and furnished in the Chinese style. Hand-painted peacocks, chrysanthemums, and pagodas adorned the green silk walls, and a specially woven carpet covered the floor in a swirl of water lilies. There were chairs and sofas upholstered in figured golden velvet, tables inlaid with different woods, and lacquered glass-fronted cabinets containing displays of porcelain, jade, and ivory. More lifesize figures stood against the walls, this time of Chinese fishermen carrying unlit jade lamps, and the crystal chandeliers suspended from the coffered ceiling had been made to resemble Oriental lanterns. Only one of the chandeliers had been lit, and this, together with the glow from the fireplace, was the only light in the room. The golden velvet curtains at the tall windows had been left undrawn, and the room was reflected in the polished glass. Beyond the reflection, she could just make out the street lamps in St. James's Place.

The butler bowed to her. "If you will wait here, madam . . ."

"Until Mr. Beaufort arrives? Yes, for I have little choice."

He flushed a little on realizing she'd overheard in the courtyard, and he withdrew, without another word, closing the double doors softly behind him.

Silence seemed to fold over her, so much so that she gave a start as the fire shifted suddenly. She turned quickly to look at it, and her glance was drawn to a portrait on the chimney breast above. It was a full-length figure of a breathtakingly beautiful young woman with shining dark curls, a heart-shaped face, and magnificent lilac eyes. She wore a pale-pink satin gown, and the scene in the background was of an elegant country mansion set high on a hillside. The whole was set against an ominous, thundery sky, after the style of Mr. Gainsborough. It was a very fine portrait indeed. Rosalind knew without being told that it was a likeness of Celia Beaufort.

She went a little closer, studying the sweet face. This was the woman Philip had loved, but who'd been described by Mrs. Penruthin as a spiteful, selfish, disagreeable cat. What had the real Celia been like? Had she been the adorable wife Philip had believed her to be? Or was Mrs. Penruthin's description closer to the mark? Rosalind gazed at the exquisite figure, remembering what else the Cornishwoman had said. Had handsome Dom Rodrigo de Freire been more than just a friend to Lady Southvale?

As Rosalind studied the painting, she knew a faint feeling of hurt, for she was about to become the second Lady Southvale, and yet this arresting portrait of Philip's first wife was still placed in a very prominent position in the house. Rosalind turned away, wondering again why Philip had apparently not said anything of his new betrothal. He'd mentioned it at the Black Horse, there was no doubt of that, but here in London no one seemed to know anything about her. Why? She glanced unwillingly at the portrait again, and then quickly away. Had he returned here, looked once more at Celia's likeness, and known that after all he was still too much in love with her to contemplate going through with a second marriage? Was that how it had been? But even as she thought this, a further possibility occurred to her. Had he come back to London and found another new love? Had someone else stolen his heart so completely that everything in Washington was relegated to little more than a passing diversion?

She heard a carriage approaching along St. James's Place and went to the window to look out. The carriage lamps swung as the vehicle turned in between the gates of the house. She wondered briefly if it could be Lady Eleanor and Miss de Grey returning, but then she caught a fleeting glimpse of a gentleman seated alone inside. It had to be the Mr. Beaufort the butler had sent for.

Hesitating for just a moment, she suddenly gathered her skirts to hurry to the doors, intending to go out on to the gallery to look down into the entrance hall. As she reached the balustrade, she heard someone rapping peremptorily on the door with a cane.

The butler hastened to admit the caller. "Forgive me for sending for you, Mr. Beaufort, but I didn't know what else to do."

Mr. Beaufort strode in, his cloak swirling as he turned to face the butler. "What in God's name is all this about, Richardson? That fool you sent said something about a woman who claims she's going to be the next Lady South-vale."

Rosalind leaned over, trying to see the newcomer's face, but he wore a top hat that was pulled well forward, and he made no move to take it off.

The butler was evidently very unhappy about having had to send for this particular gentleman. "I'm truly sorry, Mr. Beaufort, but there is indeed such a lady. She's American, and I've admitted her to the drawing room."

Mr. Beaufort gave an incredulous laugh. "You've actually allowed the creature in? Dammit, man, don't you know a fortune-seeker when you see one?"

"I'm not sure she is a fortune-seeker, sir, for she's wearing his lordship's signet ring."

There was a moment's startled silence. "Are you sure it's his ring?"

"Oh, yes, Mr. Beaufort, and I have noticed that he hasn't been wearing it since his return."

"Yes, that's true," mumured the other.

"I fear the lady may indeed be what she claims to be, sir."

"Then why hasn't he said anything about her? No, Richardson, she isn't his new betrothed, I think we may be

quite sure of that. I don't profess to know how she came
by his ring, but it's my guess that she's an adventuress, no
more and no less.''

On the floor above, Rosalind listened with increasing
dismay, disliking the arrogant, unpleasant Mr. Beaufort more
with each insulting word he uttered. How dared he say such
things about her without even having set eyes upon her!

Richardson was still uneasy about everything, and not as
certain as Mr. Beaufort that the unwelcome arrival from
America was there under false pretenses. ''Sir, by her
manner and dress, Miss Carberry is most definitely a lady,
and she's brought her luggage with her.'' He turned to
indicate the cases and valises nearby.

Mr. Beaufort hadn't noticed them before, but wasn't
impressed. ''That doesn't signify anything. Besides, I can
tell you very certainly that she isn't going to become the next
lady Southvale.''

''But—''

''It's quite out of the question,'' interrupted the other. ''In
fact, it's quite impossible.''

Rosalind gazed down at him in puzzlement. How could
he say that? It was almost as if he knew something.

Richardson looked curiously at him too, but then drew a
long breath. ''That's as may be, Mr. Beaufort, but there's
still the matter of the ring. She's wearing it on the fourth
finger of her left hand, and as his lordship hasn't said anything about losing the ring, I have to wonder if he did indeed
give it to her. I don't know where he is at the moment, and
Lady Eleanor and Miss de Grey are out at dinner, so I thought
it best to send for you. You are family, sir, well, more or
less . . .''

''Very well, Richardson, since you've sent for me, I'll deal
with the matter. She's in the drawing room, you say?''

''Yes, sir.''

Mr. Beaufort turned for the butler to assist him with his
cloak, and Rosalind drew back immediately from the
balustrade, returning quickly to the drawing room. She sat

down on a sofa close to the fireplace, arranging her gown and pelisse as if she'd been sitting there ever since she'd first been shown in. Her heart had begun to beat more swiftly, for she knew that there wasn't going to be anything amicable about her meeting with Mr. Beaufort. He was going to "deal" with her, and from his manner so far, that could only mean a hostile confrontation.

Swift steps crossed the landing from the top of the staircase, and she steeled herself as the doors were flung unceremoniously open. The first thing she realized about Mr. Beaufort as he strode in was that he was far too young to be Celia's father, for he was somewhere in his late twenties or early thirties. Perhaps he was her cousin. He was a little above medium height, but not tall, and rather sensuously good-looking. His wavy hair was dark-chestnut in color, and his long-lashed eyes were hazel, so that he didn't resemble the late Lady Southvale in any way whatsoever. His lips were well-shaped, but pressed angrily together, and there was something intentionally intimidating about the way he halted before Rosalind, his cold, rather disparaging glance sweeping her from head to toe. Now that he'd discarded his cloak, she saw that the clothes beneath were very elegant and fashionable. He wore a black corded-silk coat, white silk breeches, a white satin waistcoat, and a frilled shirt. There was a diamond pin sparkling in the folds of his complicated neckcloth, and he looked every inch the London gentleman of quality, except that there was nothing even remotely gentlemanly in his manner toward her.

"Miss Carberry, I believe," he said coolly.

"Mr. Beaufort, I believe," she replied in a tone equally as cool, for she disliked him intensely, and was determined to hide how vulnerable and alone she felt.

"I'm told you claim to be Philip's future wife."

"You're told correctly."

He went to a small table upon which stood a decanter and a number of glasses. As he poured himself a generous measure of cognac, he glanced deliberately toward the portrait above the fireplace. "Do you really imagine you can replace my sister, Miss Carberry?"

His sister? So that's who he was.

He turned to face her again, the glass swirling in his hand. "I asked you a question, madam."

"I know you did, sir, but I don't particullarly care for your tone. The fact that you are Lady Southvale's brother does not give you the right to be disgracefully rude to me."

A light passed through his hazel eyes, and a faintly contemptuous smile touched his lips. "My, my, how very grand you are, to be sure."

"And how very blackguardly you are. To be sure." She held his gaze, thinking that he was surely the most disagreeable person it had ever been her misfortune to meet. If his late sister had been anything like him, then it was certain that Mrs. Penruthin's description of Celia Beaufort had been the right one.

"I don't have to be anything else, madam, for you aren't going to be the next Lady Southvale, and you've wasted your time coming here."

"I have Philip's ring to prove my claim," she replied, holding up her hand.

"You could have come by that in any number of ways, Miss Carberry."

"All of them felonious, no doubt."

He gave a faint smile and raised the glass to his lips.

She smiled too, and in equally as insulting a manner. "Well, sir, I don't really have to worry what you think, do I? You aren't the master of this house."

His smile faded abruptly and his eyes flashed. "I don't claim to be the master here, madam, but nevertheless I've been sent for to deal with you!"

"How very tiresome for you. I'm so sorry to have dragged you away from the green baize. If you were in any way a proper gentleman, I'd express my apologies for having gotten between you and your pleasure, but since you're anything but a gentleman, I'm really quite glad to have ruined your evening.''

''Enjoy your gladness while you can, madam, for you aren't going to be here for very long. You aren't going to marry Philip de Grey, and if you take my advice, you'll leave this house immediately.''

Before Rosalind could reply, a woman's rather imperious voice interrupted them.

''What is going on here? I demand to be told immediately!''

They both looked quickly toward the door. Two elegantly dressed ladies stood there. One was gray-haired and elderly, the other was about Rosalind's own age, dark-haired and shyly pretty, with eyes of a very similar blue to Philip's. They could only be his great-aunt, Lady Eleanor Laird, and his sister, Miss Katherine de Grey.

12

Lady Eleanor advanced into the room. She was slightly built and very patrician, with a delicately boned face and haughty eyes. A few carefully arranged wisps of gray hair peeped from beneath her coffee satin turban, and her long-sleeved, high-waisted gown was made of the same satin. She wore brown lace fingerless mittens, and there was a warm rose-and-white cashmere shawl around her shoulders.

Katherine de Grey remained by the doorway. She was taller than her great-aunt, with a pleasingly rounded figure. Her gown was made of white brocade, short-sleeved and square-necked, and there was a golden belt at its high waist, immediately beneath her breasts. Her elbow-length gloves were aquamarine, embroidered in gold, and an aquamarine feather boa was draped lightly over her arms. She wore her long brown hair *à l'égyptienne*, with a golden headband from which sprang a flouncy white plume. She gazed at Rosalind for a long moment and then lowered her eyes to the floor.

Lady Eleanor's closed fan tapped against her palm as she too surveyed Rosalind, but then she looked at Mr. Beaufort. "Well, sir?"

"Has Richardson explained anything?" he asked in reply.

"He told me of the arrival of an American lady who is

making some rather startling claims concerning Philip.''

Mr. Beaufort made a faint gesture toward Rosalind, shrugging and raising his eyebrows as he did so. ''The lady in question,'' he murmured.

Lady Eleanor looked at Rosalind again. ''I understand that your name is Miss Carberry.''

''Yes, and I suppose Philip hasn't mentioned me to you, either,'' replied Rosalind with a heavy heart.

The old lady pursed her lips. ''No, he hasn't.''

Rosalind glanced at Katherine de Grey, who was now her only hope. ''Do you know anything about me, Miss de Grey?''

''No, I'm afraid I don't.''

Mr. Beaufort drained his glass. ''Which all seems a little strange, don't you agree? This, er, lady sports Philip's signet ring and says he asked her to marry him, but not a single word has passed his lips on the subject. She's quite obviously trying it on.''

Lady Eleanor's lips twitched. ''Trying it on? And what, pray, does that mean?''

He endeavored to conceal his irritation. ''It means that she's a fraud,'' he replied shortly.

''All this newfangled vocabulary,'' she muttered disapprovingly, her fan still tapping. Then she eyed him. ''Well, sir, since you quite obviously do not believe Miss Carberry's story, I suppose I can understand your attitude, but understanding it and condoning it are two entirely different matters. You were being grossly offensive when I arrived, and I find that totally unacceptable.''

A quick flush touched his cheeks. ''Lady Eleanor, the woman is an adventuress.''

''In your opinion.''

''If she isn't, why hasn't Philip said anything about her?'' he demanded.

She breathed out slowly. ''That I cannot say.''

''She isn't about to become Lady Southvale, so what point is there in pretending?''

Rosalind looked sharply at him again. He really did seem very certain about her fate. Why? Was it solely because Philip hadn't mentioned her, or did he know something?

Lady Eleanor studied him. "We don't know that she isn't telling the truth, sir, nor do we know that she isn't about to replace Celia. While Philip remains so stubbornly and inexplicably absent from the arena, we can't know anything at all, and so it rather ill becomes you to adopt such an irredeemable attitude. Philip may no longer be your brother-in-law—strictly speaking, that is—but he is still your good friend, and it just may be that he intends to marry Miss Carberry, so might it not be more prudent for you to follow my example and reserve judgment?"

He pressed his lips angrily together, and a nerve flickered at his temple. He turned abruptly away and poured himself another liberal glass of Philip's cognac.

Lady Eleanor sighed and went to sit on a chair opposite Rosalind. Katherine went to stand behind her great-aunt, a hand resting slightly on the back of the chair. Rosalind felt very much under scrutiny, as if there were four people endeavoring to assess her honesty: Lady Eleanor, Miss de Grey, Mr. Beaufort, and Celia herself, whose painted face seemed to be gazing down from the wall.

Lady Eleanor looked at her. "Tell me, Miss Carberry, how long have you known my great-nephew?"

"Since the evening of the Fourth of July."

"That's very precise."

"Yes."

"I happen to know that he left Washington toward the end of August, which doesn't leave very long for your acquaintance to have developed."

Rosalind couldn't hide an ironic smile. "Lady Eleanor, we met on the Fourth of July, and he proposed to me on the fifth of July. Our wedding was arranged for the end of August, but he was suddenly sent back here three days before."

Her words fell into a stunned silence, and it was Mr.

Beaufort who recovered first. He gave a disparaging laugh. "Such an instant flame of passion? So vibrant and undeniable *affaire de coeur*? And yet Philip hasn't felt it necessary to inform us about it? How very curious."

Rosalind lowered her eyes, for Philip's inexplicable silence was very disquieting.

Lady Eleanor spoke again. "Miss Carberry, do you have any proof of your claim, other than your possession of the signet ring?"

Rosalind raised her eyes reluctantly. "Not with me. He did write to me from Falmouth, but I left the letter at home in Washington."

Mr. Beaufort studied his glass. "How very convenient," he murmured.

Lady Eleanor shot him a dark glance and then returned her attention to Rosalind. "There is nothing else?"

Rosalind thought for a moment. "He told Mr. and Mrs. Penruthin about me."

"Mr. and Mrs. Penruthin?" repeated the old lady, the names evidently meaning nothing to her.

Katherine leaned down to her. "Mr. Penruthin is the landlord at the inn in Falmouth, Great-aunt. He's known Philip for quite a long time."

"I see." Lady Eleanor looked at Rosalind again. "And this Mr. Penruthin therefore knows about you?"

"Yes."

Lady Eleanor studied her. "We could, of course, approach these people in Falmouth, but that would take over a week, and I expect Philip to return in that time. He has a very important meeting at the Foreign Office, concerning his forthcoming assignment in St. Petersburg, and the only thing we do know about his movements is that he intends to be back here in time to keep that appointment. Miss Carberry, is there any other way that your claims can be substantiated?"

"Well, Signora Segati knows about me. She was staying at the inn and I drove to London in her chaise. I know that Mrs. Penruthin told her why I was in England."

A rather disapproving expression descended over the old lady's face. "Signora Segati? The opera singer?"

"Yes, that's right."

"I see." The words were uttered very tersely.

Mr. Beaufort gave a dry chuckle. "My dear Miss Carberry, Segati is renowned as being one of the most incurable fibbers in Christendom. Her powers of invention are as legendary as her voice, and no one in their right mind would accept anything she said without taking a very large pinch of salt. How very appropriate that you should drop her name, for, to be sure, you and she are birds of a feather."

"Mr. Beaufort," snapped Lady Eleanor angrily. "Unless you desist, I shall have you removed from the house!"

"But—"

"One more word and I shall ring for Richardson," she threatened.

He sighed and said nothing more.

Lady Eleanor looked at Rosalind. "My dear, Signora Segati isn't an ideal witness for your defense, for she is indeed an inveterate teller of tall tales. The last time she was in London, she told everyone that the Duke of Wellington was going to divorce his duchess in order to marry her, but it turned out that the duke hadn't even met her, let alone proposed marriage. So, you see, I can hardly approach her on the matter of your claims concerning Philip." She paused for a long moment. "No, there's only one thing for it: you must stay here at Southvale House until Philip returns."

Mr. Beaufort was appalled. "Lady Eleanor, you can't possibly be serious."

"I'm not in the habit of jesting, sir," she replied in a chilly tone.

"But to invite her to stay beneath this roof! Surely it would be wiser to find her a room at a suitable establishment? Grillion's, for example?"

"I hardly think that is a very sensible idea, sir," replied the old lady coldly. "What if Philip confirms everything Miss

Carberry has said? The whole of London will then learn that we declined to offer a welcome to the next Lady Southvale. That won't do at all.''

Katherine de Grey suddenly spoke to Rosalind. "Miss Carberry, you said that you met Philip on the Fourth of July. Would you mind telling me where?''

Rosalind was a little surprised at the question. "It was at a ball at my home, my parents throw a grand ball every year on that day, it's become quite a social tradition.''

"Will you describe the outside of your home?''

"The outside?'' Rosalind was a little taken aback. "Well, it's a large house in the classical style, and it's known locally as the Carberry mansion. It's set in its own grounds, but the specimen trees my father chose aren't very well established yet. They will be soon, though, and then it will all look much better. There's a terrace overlooking my mother's rose garden . . .''

Katherine smiled suddenly. "With a little summerhouse?''

"Yes.''

Katherine looked at Mr. Beaufort. "I think you may have to eat your words, Gerald, because Philip told me about that night. I asked him about Washington society, and about Washington itself, and he said that some of the houses there were as grand as anything here in London. He also told me about attending a Fourth of July ball at one particular mansion, and he mentioned the rose garden, because he knows how much I love roses. He was very strange when he told me about that night, and he said that it was one of the most important and momentous occasions of his life. Of course it was, for he met Miss Carberry!''

Rosalind felt a surge of relief, for at least one person here now believed her. But her relief was short-lived, for Gerald's next words reminded her of one salutary fact: Philip had chosen not to mention her to anyone.

Gerald faced Katherine. "If it was so important and momentous because of Miss Carberry, why in God's name didn't he say so? Why all the mystery? Why not simply inform us all that he intended to marry her? Well? What explanation have you got for that, Katherine?''

She lowered her eyes. ''I haven't got one,'' she replied reluctantly. ''All I know is that one moment he was on top of the world, the next he was so sunk in gloom and despondency that I was quite alarmed. Well, perhaps it wasn't quite like that. I was on my own here when he returned, and I rushed out to greet him when he got out of his carriage. He was happier than I'd ever seen him before. He swung me up in the air and told me he had something wonderful to tell me, but that first of all he'd attend to whatever letters had arrived for him during his absence. He told me to have tea served here in the drawing room, because he wouldn't be long, he'd just check that there wasn't anything of pressing importance. When he joined me in here, he was very quiet and low, different in every way from the man who'd arrived shortly before. I tried to make him smile, but it was impossible, and that's when I asked him about Washington.''

Gerald shrugged. ''Anyway, it's all academic, because I can tell you quite categorically that Philip isn't going to marry again.''

Katherine was vexed with him. ''The trouble with you, Gerald Beaufort, is that you don't find it easy to admit you're wrong. Miss Carberry isn't an adventuress or a fortune-seeker, she's a lady from a very wealthy background, and such ladies don't leave their homes for no good reason. She's come here to marry Philip, and has his ring to prove it, which is good enough for me when set beside what he said about the Fourth of July.''

Lady Eleanor nodded. ''I'm more than inclined to agree with you, Katherine. It's settled then, Miss Carberry will stay here with us until Philip returns and sheds some light upon the mystery. Miss Carberry, I take it you've brought your maid with you?''

''Well, I did, but she fell ill with a fever during the voyage and has remained in Falmouth with the Penruthins.''

The old lady looked up at Katherine. "Celia's maid, Annie, was kept on, wasn't she?"

"Yes, Great-aunt. She never accompanied Celia on visits, and Philip didn't think it right to dismiss her. She's been with us ever since."

"Ring for Richardson, if you please. The pagoda room must be put at our guest's disposal, and Annie must be instructed to wait upon her."

As Katherine went to pick up the little silver bell on a nearby table, Lady Eleanor gave Gerald a firm look. "Now, then, sirrah, I don't wish to hear any more argument from you. Miss Carberry is to be my guest, and unless you're prepared to be civil, I suggest you keep away from this house for the time being. Do I make myself clear?"

Gerald hesitated, but then sketched an elegantly acquiescent bow. "I promise to be the personification of civility, Lady Eleanor," he murmured.

"See that you are," she replied tartly.

Rosalind had lowered her gaze to the fire. Well, one way or another she was to be made welcome in Philip's house, but it wasn't the way she wished it to be. She was desperately worried as to why Philip had omitted to tell anyone about her, and she wished Hetty was with her, instead of two hundred and fifty miles away in Cornwall.

Suddenly she raised her eyes and found herself looking into Gerald's almost speculative gaze. He didn't glance away, but gave a slight smile, raising his glass to her.

13

❧

Rosalind was too unsettled and worried to sleep well that first night in London. She lay awake for long periods, and when she slept, her dreams were disturbing. But it was the one she had just before being awakened by Celia's maid, Annie, that disturbed her most of all, for it was so real that it could have been happening.

She was riding to meet Philip by the fallen tree near her Washington home. Her heart was racing and there were tears in her eyes. She wanted to ride faster, but something seemed to be holding her back, and the horse moved at no more than a very slow canter.

All around her the green summer woods were touched with gold by the setting sun, and shadows lay like bars across her path. The insect noise she remembered so well was throbbing all around, in time to the frantic pounding of her heart. A single thought consumed her: please let Philip be there as he'd promised, please let him be able to tell her everything was still all right.

She could hear John calling after her. "I'd never have brought him near the house if I'd realized this would happen." A sob caught in her throat. Should she be listening to her brother, or to her heart, which urged her on into the woods?

John called again. "He means nothing but heartbreak for you, Sis . . . nothing but heartbreak." Heartbreak, heartbreak, heartbreak . . . The calls died away like an echo and became lost in the insect noise.

The fallen tree was visible ahead now, and Philip was waiting, the reins of his horse swinging idly in his gloved hand as he leaned back against the trunk. He turned as he heard her, and his eyes were very blue and forceful. As she reined in before him, he came to lift her down to the ground. He smiled, but his fingers were hard and cruel, pinching her through the soft material of her riding habit. His smile didn't reach his eyes, and he was strangely different, as if the real Philip de Grey had gone, and someone else was there instead.

"Philip, you're hurting me," she protested.

"Forgive me, Rosalind, for the last thing I wish to do is upset you." They were words he'd really said to her in those woods, but in the dream they were cold and without feeling.

She searched his face, desperate for the reassurance that would sweep aside her deep uncertainty. "Do you still love me, Philip?" she asked.

"I love you, Rosalind, and have done so from the very first moment I saw you." More remembered words, but hollow now.

"Do you promise?"

"I want you to be my wife, to become the second Lady Southvale, and to come back to England with me."

"I'm afraid, Philip."

"Marry me, Rosalind."

"Oh, Philip, of course I'll marry you."

He smiled again, but although his lips were inviting, his eyes were remote. He pulled her close, bending his head to kiss her. It was a hard, relentless kiss, another distortion of the reality she'd known before, but it was skillful, coaxing an unwilling response from her treacherous senses. As a lover he had no equal, but he was using her for his own pleasure, with no thought of her. She suddenly knew that she meant nothing to him, in spite of his honeyed words, but still her deceitful body responded to his touch. She was powerless to resist as a rich, voluptuous warmth spread beguilingly through her. A low moan escaped her bruised but wanton lips, but even as she surrendered, he suddenly thrust her aside.

"What a fool you are, Rosalind," he said scathingly, "believing all I told you, and questioning nothing." There was nothing remembered about his words now, they were painfully new and uncompromising.

He turned away, leaving her as he walked toward the trees. Then she saw Celia. She was dressed in the same pale-pink satin gown as the portrait, and there was a mocking smile on her sweet lips as she turned to look at her vanquished American rival.

Philip's fingers closed lovingly over his wife's. The sun went in and a low rumble of thunder spread ominously across the darkening skies. Then the insects fell abruptly silent.

After a moment there was a new sound, a hissing sound that had no place there. Rosalind woke up with a start and then realized that the noise was the drawing back of the curtains on a new morning. Annie was by the windows, and once the blue velvet curtains had been tied back by their ropes, she folded back the shutters. Morning light flooded into the room.

Rosalind watched her for a moment. The maid was small and thin, with brown hair that she wore back in a very tight knot beneath her starched mobcap. Her face was pale and plain, with a scattering of freckles over the nose, and she wore a fawn linen gown that did little to assist her rather drab appearance. She seemed to be of a rather morose disposition, but was very capable and efficient, coming to the bedside the moment she saw that her new mistress was awake.

"Good morning, madam."

"Good morning, Annie."

"I've brought you your morning cup of tea." The maid indicated the little table by the bed.

''Thank you.'' The influence of the dream was still around Rosalind, but she made herself sit up in the immense four-poster bed.

Annie immediately brought her a warm shawl, which she placed around Rosalind's shoulders. ''The fire's been attended to, madam, but it will be a little while before it heats the room up properly.'' The maid picked up the cup of tea and put it carefully in Rosalind's hands.

Sipping the tea, Rosalind glanced around at her new surroundings. The room was called the pagoda room not only because of the shoulder-high porcelain pagodas that stood on either side of the fireplace and the windows, but also because the bluebell muslin canopy of the bed had been cleverly fashioned to resemble a Chinese roof. The porcelain pagodas were hollow, with latticework panels, so that lighted candles could be placed inside. They'd been lit the night before and had cast pretty shadows over the blue hand-painted silk on the walls. There were tall mirrors on the walls, the glass carved with borders of peonies, and a particularly ornate cheval glass stood in one corner, its frame adorned with gilded dragons. Two bamboo armchairs stood on either side of the fireplace, their cushions made of the same bluebell velvet as the curtains at the windows, and there was a dressing table covered with frilled white muslin. Through an adjoining doorway there was a dressing room containing a washstand and several wardrobes.

The newly tended fire crackled and spat, but was already beginning to warm the room. Rosalind glanced toward the windows. She could just see the tops of the trees in Green Park, for the room was on the third floor. She'd looked out the evening before, and although it had been dark, she'd been able to see a wide terrace below, where the view of the park could be enjoyed. The distant noise of Piccadilly could be heard, but closer to the house, somewhere in the park, a flower girl was calling.

Annie put some more coals on the fire and then returned

to the bed. "Which gown would you like me to put out, madam?"

"The green dimity, I think," replied Rosalind, wishing she'd brought a more varied wardrobe with her from Washington.

"Yes, madam."

The maid hurried away to the dressing room, and Rosalind watched her. Annie was very efficient, she thought again, but lacked that warmth that had set Hetty aside. She spoke politely enough and attended assiduously to her duties, but there was definitely something lacking in her manner. And if only she'd *smile* once in a while!

Annie brought the green dimity and put it carefully over one of the bamboo chairs by the fireplace so that it wouldn't be too chill when Rosalind put it on. "Will you use the green-and-white shawl with it, madam?" she asked then.

"Yes."

The maid turned to go back to the dressing room.

"Annie . . ."

"Madam?"

"Is there any word from Lord Southvale?"

"No, madam."

Rosalind hid her disappointment. She hadn't really expected any other reply, but had hoped all the same. If no one knew where Philip had been for the past few weeks, it wasn't really very likely now that he'd return much before his appointment at the Foreign Office. She glanced at the clock on the mantelpiece and then at the maid again. "When will breakfast be served?"

"In half an hour's time, madam. Lady Eleanor has already gone out, for she is to take breakfast with friends this morning, but Miss Katherine is in and will join you on the terrace."

Rosalind was startled. "On the terrace?"

"Yes, madam."

"But isn't it a little cold?"

"There is a little rotunda, madam, with windows all

around, and a fireplace. It is always used for breakfast if the weather is fine." The maid went into the dressing room again and returned with the shawl, which she placed to warm with the gown. "Mr. Beaufort will call later this morning, madam," she said, coming to the bedside again.

Rosalind lowered her cup, wondering why the maid had told her. "Really?" she replied, in a tone that was meant to convey her complete disinterest in that gentleman's activities.

"Yes, madam, for it's been agreed that he will escort you today."

"Escort me?" Rosalind didn't like the sound of it.

"Yes, madam. Lady Eleanor thought you would like to see the sights of London while she and Miss Katherine were otherwise engaged today, and so she requested Mr. Beaufort to wait upon you. I am to accompany you as well, so that all will be proper."

The thought of being escorted by Gerald Beaufort was disagreeable in the extreme, for although he'd endeavored to honor his word to Lady Eleanor and had been the soul of civility during the remainder of the previous evening, the memory of his earlier conduct lingered. He really had been grossly rude and insulting, and that wasn't something Rosalind was prepared to forget in a hurry. He was totally unacceptable to her, and she had no intention of allowing him to escort her anywhere. A suitably indestructible excuse would have to be thought up.

About half an hour later, Annie led her down through the house to the terrace. The morning air was cold and fresh as they emerged outside, and Rosalind drew the shawl closer. The little rotunda occupied the southwest corner of the terrace, and its windows shone in the morning sun. A curl of smoke rose into the air from the tiny chimney, and as Rosalind drew closer, she could see the white-clothed table inside and the bowl of red chrysanthemums that had been placed in the middle. Gold-and-white porcelain caught the sunlight, and silver cutlery gleamed; it looked very inviting and pleasant, and she thought it all an excellent idea.

There was no sign as yet of Katherine, and so Rosalind waited inside, gazing out over the park. The autumn colors were magnificent, for it was one of the leafiest parks she had ever seen. She was to learn that this was because the Tyburn stream passed below its surface, and it was consequently always well-watered. The park was roughly triangular in shape, and of an undulating character, with two shallow hills toward the center. It was bounded by Piccadilly to the north, and she could see a narrow, rectangular sheet of water by the park wall. To the south she could see the avenues of trees marking the commencement of the Mall, while to the southwest there was Constitution Hill and Buckingham House, a royal residence. There were gravel paths, but no flower beds, and almost in the very center, barely visible because of the trees, she could see a mound on which stood the remains of a very old building. She was later to be told that this was King Charles the Second's icehouse, for that convivial monarch had liked his wine chilled in the summer months.

As she stood there, a sudden movement almost directly below the terrace caught her attention. She looked down to see a postern gate in the wall bounding the property of Southvale House. A gardener was carrying a large terra-cotta pot containing an ornamental bay tree, and as she watched, he placed it very carefully beside the gravel path that led from the gate toward a wide walk that passed from north to south through the park. Other bay trees had already been carried out, and lined the path like sentries, and then she saw that other potted plants had been carried out into the park: ferns, citrus trees, and little conifers. The gardener returned through the postern gate, wiping his hands on his sacking apron, and he disappeared into a little stone building in the lee of the wall. A moment or so later he came out with another bay tree.

A voice spoke suddenly from the doorway of the rotunda.

"As you can see, Miss Carberry, we have our own private access to the park."

Rosalind turned quickly to see Katherine standing there, the orange ribbons in her little lace day bonnet fluttering a little as a stray draft swept momentarily over the terrace. She wore a cream gown and carried an orange-and-brown shawl. She smiled and closed the rotunda door.

"I hope you haven't been waiting for long."

"No, not long."

"Did you sleep well?"

"Yes," replied Rosalind untruthfully.

"I'm so glad, for there's nothing more disagreeable than a poor night after a long and tiring journey." Katherine hesitated. "To say nothing of a less-than-warm welcome," she added.

Rosalind looked out of the window again. "I cannot deny that my arrival was greeted with some coolness."

"That's putting it mildly. You mustn't take any notice of Gerald, for he isn't of importance, not anymore, anyway. And I believe what you've told us."

"I know you do, and I'm very grateful."

Katherine came to stand next to her. "I think Philip intended to tell us about you, but that something happened."

"What do you think it might have been?"

Katherine sighed. "I don't know. As I said last night, he was all smiles and happiness when he arrived, and then, all of a sudden, he was sunk as low as when news of Celia's death reached us. Forgive me, it's not really the thing to speak of Celia to you, is it?"

"I cannot ignore the fact that she existed."

"No, I suppose not."

Rosalind studied her, for Katherine de Grey reminded her of someone. But who?

Katherine wasn't aware of the perusal. "There must have been something in one of the letters that were waiting for him, I can't see that it could have been anything else. It upset me to see him suddenly so unhappy, and I really did my best to cheer him up. As I said, I tried to make him tell me about Washington, and that's when he described the ball at your home. It was just after that that he ordered . . ." Katherine broke off, coloring a little and lowering her eyes.

"That he ordered what?" prompted Rosalind curiously.

"It doesn't matter."

Rosalind looked intently at her. "I think it does, Miss de Grey. Please tell me what you were about to say."

Katherine drew a reluctant breath. "Very well. He ordered Celia's portrait to be returned to the drawing room."

Rosalind's lips parted briefly and she turned her head quickly away.

Katherine's voice continued unhappily. "Just before he left for America, he had the portrait removed to Celia's rooms, for he said it made him feel sad to look at it."

Rosalind didn't know what to say or what to think. Yesterday she'd begun to suspect that Philip had changed his mind about marrying for a second time because he was surrounded by memories of his beloved first wife. Now it seemed that that suspicion may prove correct. She couldn't help a wry, ironic smile, for she remembered what she'd been dreaming when Annie had awakened her. In the dream Philip had discarded her because of Celia, and from what she'd now learned from Katherine, it was a dream that could easily become reality.

Katherine touched her arm apologetically. "I'm sorry if what I've said has upset you."

"I did insist upon being told," Rosalind reminded her. She gave a slight smile. "Perhaps I'd have been wiser to have listened to my brother . . ." She broke off, suddenly remembering who it was that Katherine resembled. It was Elizabeth Mackintosh, who would have married John had it not been for the accident.

Katherine looked at her in concern. "Is something wrong, Miss Carberry?"

"No, it's just that you've been reminding me of someone, and I couldn't think who it was. I've just realized that you're very like my brother's late fiancée, Miss Mackintosh. He loved her very much, and even though it's more than a year since she died, he's still not over her.'' Rosalind smiled ruefully. ''Perhaps he and Philip aren't that much unalike, after all,'' she murmured.

Katherine understood her meaning. ''Because Philip has had Celia's portrait returned to the drawing room, and it's well over a year since she died, too?''

''Yes, I suppose so.''

''Miss Carberry, if Philip loved you enough to ask you to marry him, then you may take my word for it that he's recovered from any grief he felt over Celia.'' Katherine gave a rather irritated sigh. ''Oh, how I loathed her! She was the very worst thing that ever happened to my brother.''

Rosalind's eyes widened. ''I beg your pardon?'' she said.

''I loathed Celia, and she loathed me. Believe me, it was thoroughly mutual, although Philip never realized it. She never put a foot wrong in front of him, but when he wasn't there, she was a *chienne*. I didn't shed any tears when I learned she was dead.''

Rosalind stared at her, for the conversation suddenly contained very clear echoes of another conversation, with Mrs. Penruthin at the Black Horse in Falmouth.

Katherine smiled, a little amused by Rosalind's obvious astonishment. ''I see no reason to pretend about Celia, Miss Carberry, for apart from always having been a difficult and at times unpleasant sister-in-law, she was also responsible for the singularly most wretched experience in my life. Did Philip ever tell you that I'd had an unhappy love affair?''

''Well, yes, he did mention it, but not in any detail.''

''I was a fool, I loved too much and too unwisely. Celia deliberately introduced him to a fascinating widowed countess who made me seem dull, and he left me for her. Celia did it simply to cause me as much pain as she could. She wrongly thought I was to blame because Philip refused to buy her a diamond necklace she particularly wanted, but I hadn't said anything to him, he'd decided against it because he heard that the Duke of Newbridge was taking legal action to reclaim it from the jeweler, because it was supposed to have been stolen from Newbridge Place two years ago. Celia decided it was all my fault, though, and her subsequent actions were based on nothing more than spite. It all happened just before she left that last time for Ireland, and I was so miserably unhappy that poor Philip became quite anxious about me. Of all things, he tried to make her stay behind to comfort me!'' Katherine gave a short laugh. ''She was the last person on earth I wished to have around me, and I was glad when she insisted on going. Miss Carberry, I've never let him know how much I disliked her, and I would be grateful if you wouldn't tell him.''

''Of course I won't.''

''If you don't mind my saying so, although you are obviously surprised at my candidness, you don't seem surprised at what I've actually said about Celia.''

Rosalind lowered her eyes for a moment. ''Mrs. Penruthin also told me what my predecessor was really like. Celia wasn't exactly popular at the Black Horse.''

''I thought something must have happened there when she suddenly took to staying at a different inn. I didn't believe her that it was just because it was more convenient to be down by the quay. What happened?''

Rosalind told her, but without mentioning Dom Rodrigo and the rides on the moors.

Katherine sighed. ''Demanding a poor stableboy's punishment? That sounds just like dear Celia. Oh, I still can't believe that she so successfully pulled the wool over Philip's eyes.''

''Love is blind, or so they say.''

They were silent for a long moment, and then Rosalind remembered that Gerald was supposed to be calling later. ''Annie tells me that Mr. Beaufort is going to wait upon me later this morning.''

''Yes. It was my great-aunt's idea.''

"Not one of her better ones," murmured Rosalind with feeling.

Katherine gave her a wicked glance. "But he's so charming and pleasing," she said, her tongue firmly in her cheek.

"I'd as soon be in the company of a snake."

Katherine laughed. "Well, I have to admit that I'd feel the same way, if I were you. But I also have to concede that last night he did seem to have repented, and he gladly agreed to my great-aunt's suggestion."

"Gladly? I find that hard to believe," replied Rosalind, recalling how extremely unpleasant he'd been when he'd first confronted her.

"He'd been called away from a winning hand, and gentlemen with mountainous gambling debts don't take too kindly to such interference."

"That doesn't excuse him." Rosalind paused. "It's strange, but several times last night, when he insisted that Philip wouldn't marry again, I felt almost as if he knew something I didn't."

"I know, I thought the same. He can't know anything, though, because Philip and he didn't meet when Philip returned from Washington. Philip was only in London for a day or so, and then he simply vanished."

"Hasn't anyone any idea where he might be?"

"No. I did wonder if he was at Greys, but when I sent a message there, Mrs. Simmons, the housekeeper, sent word back that she hadn't seen him at all. He could be anywhere, and it's just not like him to be so thoughtless."

Rosalind looked seriously at her. "Miss de Grey, why do you think he hasn't said anything about me?"

Katherine met her gaze. "I really don't know, Miss Carberry, I only wish I did. Since he returned from America he's behaved in a way that's totally out of character, but I'm sure he loves you. He wouldn't have given you his ring if he didn't." She turned quickly as Richardson entered, followed by three footmen carrying silver-domed dishes.

"Ah, breakfast at last. I was beginning to think we'd been forgotten."

The butler bowed apologetically. "Please forgive the delay, Miss Katherine, but I'm afraid there was a mishap in the kitchens and everything had to be cooked again." He went to draw out a chair for her, and she sat down.

Then he drew out a second chair for Rosalind, but as she took her place and unfolded her napkin, she was thinking about Katherine's reassurance that Philip still loved her. If he did, why hadn't he told his family and friends about her? And why had he had his late wife's portrait returned to a place of such prominence? They were two questions that didn't augur well for the future happiness of Miss Rosalind Carberry of Washington.

14

As Rosalind and Katherine sat down to their breakfast in London, Philip was still only five miles away at Greys, where he'd been all along. Mrs. Simmons, the housekeeper, had been instructed to reply untruthfully to Katherine's message, and all the shutters were still closed, continuing to give the impression that the house was unoccupied.

He'd been up since dawn, and was now riding slowly down through the park on one of the largest and most capricious thoroughbreds in the stables, chosen deliberately to take his mind off other things. He wore a pine-green riding coat and pale-gray cord breeches, and hadn't bothered to put on a top hat, so that the bright autumn sun shone on his coal-black hair. But for all his Bond Street elegance, he still looked and felt ragged, for sleep was proving hard to come by. The letter he'd struggled over had been written and sent, and all he could think of was the unhappiness with which it would be read. A nerve flickered at his temple, and his lips pressed into a firm line as he kicked his heels, suddenly urging the great bay more swiftly down toward the lake.

A shy herd of red deer fled before him, veering away to his right to melt into the thick fringe of trees marking the boundary of the estate with the Hampstead road. He could just make out the lodge by the main gates, and the lodge-keeper at work in the tiny vegetable garden at the rear. The lake sparkled in the sunshine in the valley below, the blue water dotted with graceful white swans. It was lined by more trees, some of them evergreen, but most of them in the full fiery glory of autumn color. Down beyond the lake and the valley, below the invigorating air of the high heath, London stretched away into the distance, and the day was so clear that he could easily distinguish the dome of St. Paul's on the horizon.

Behind him, Greys shone white on its grassy terrace, its shuttered windows gazing blindly over the park, but he didn't look back as he reached the trees by the shore of the lake, riding through them to the water's edge. There he reined in, leaning forward slightly on the pommel and gazing across the sheet of water that looked so natural, but that had been achieved in his great-grandfather's time by the damming of a small stream. A slight miscalculation with the surveying had meant that the water crept up six feet farther than originally intended, encircling a tiny rise in the land where an old summerhouse was built in the branches of an ancient oak tree. Rather than attempt to lower the lake again, a little Chinese bridge had been built, spanning the shallow water between the shore and the newly made island, and what had commenced as a mistake had been turned into a very lovely and novel feature.

On impulse, he dismounted, leading the horse to the bridge and tethering it. Then he walked across to the little island. A barely discernible breeze played through the leaves of the oak tree, loosening some of them so that they sailed idly down to rock on the water like little orange-and-gold boats. The summerhouse had been built two hundred years before, when the original Greys had gazed down over a tree-filled valley where a stream flowed between mossy banks, and was an elegant little structure with arched, leaded windows. Half-timbered and topped by a gracefully pointed roof, it nestled comfortably among the thick, gnarled branches, approached up a winding wooden staircase that led to a little arched door.

Philip gazed up at it, noticing how faded the wood was now and how loose some of the little tiles were on the roof. He and Katherine had played there all the time when they'd been children, but it had been sadly neglected of late. Slowly he went up the wooden staircase, pausing to shake the handrail as it wobbled beneath his touch.

The arched door creaked on its rusty hinges, and a damp smell drifted out toward him. There was sudden startled fluttering, and he ducked as a frightened dove flew out past him. When he went inside, he saw that one of the windows overlooking the middle of the lake had at some time been blown open by the wind, and doves had been roosting in the summerhouse rather than the dovecote in the kitchen garden behind the house.

The vagaries of the weather had swept in through the open window, spoiling the pretty wallpaper that had once been such a delicate blend of pink and gold, but that was now a faded, nondescript stone color. Some of the paper was peeling and damp, and he noticed a loose board above the door. The floor was in need of attention, too, for not only had the doves left their mark, but some of the boards were beginning to look rotten.

His riding crop tapping against his gleaming top boot, Philip glanced sadly around. It was his fault that the little building had come to such a sorry pass, for he hadn't given it much thought for years now. Things would have to be put right and the summerhouse rebuilt completely if necessary.

Leaning a hand on the wall, he looked out of the open window. The sunlight flashed on the lake, and two swans glided silently past. He could hear the murmur of the breeze in the oak tree and the lap of the little wavelets against the shore. It was peaceful and very beautiful.

He gazed at the patterns on the water, wishing that he could stay here in seclusion forever. But he was merely putting off the inevitable, and some time soon he had to go back to London: he had no other choice. He'd never shrunk from his duty in the past, and now wasn't the time to start.

"Duty." The very word cut into him. He closed his eyes for a moment, and when he opened them again, it seemed that he could see Rosalind's face shimmering in the glittering water below.

His breath escaped slowly, and suddenly his mind was made up. He wouldn't wait until the eve of his Foreign Office appointment before returning to London, he'd go tomorrow.

Turning, he left the summerhouse and descended the staircase. His horse pricked its ears as he crossed the Chinese bridge, and soon he was riding back up through the park toward the house. Fifteen minutes later a groom set off for Southvale House with a message for Katherine and Lady Eleanor.

After breakfast, Katherine set off on the various calls she'd arranged before Rosalind's arrival, and Rosalind went back up the staircase toward her room, still trying to think of a suitable excuse not to go anywhere with Gerald.

Reaching the top of the first flight of stairs, she saw that the drawing-room doors were open. Celia's portrait faced her, the dainty figure in pale-pink satin standing out against its thundery background. Rosalind paused, staring at her predecessor's likeness. Celia's face was a sweet, delectable mask, hiding the real woman beneath. Philip believed he'd married an angel, but an angel wouldn't have set out to so deliberately break Katherine's heart, and an angel wouldn't have tried to wreak punishment upon an innocent stableboy who couldn't have been expected to know she'd changed her fickle mind about a ride.

Rosalind gazed at the portrait for a moment longer and then went to close the drawing-room doors. Gathering her green dimity skirts, she hurried on up to the floor above and along the passage toward the pagoda room. As she went inside, however, she saw Annie start guiltily from the window, dabbing a handkerchief to her tearstained eyes.

Rosalind paused in surprise. "Annie? Whatever is it?"

"Nothing, madam," said the maid quickly, striving to quell the tears.

"Do you usually cry for no good reason?" asked Rosalind, not unkindly.

"No, m-madam." The maid hung her head, her shoulders shaking.

Rosalind went to her. "Tell me about it."

"It's my mother, madam. She's been ill for a while now, and just after I'd shown you down to the terrace, my sister brought a message. Mam's worse."

"Do you wish to go to her?"

"But Lady Eleanor has instructed me to accompany you when you drive with Mr. Beaufort."

"There isn't going to be any drive if I can help it," replied Rosalind determinedly.

"There isn't?"

"No."

"Is it because you're so very tired after traveling from Cornwall?"

What an excellent excuse! Rosalind nodded. "Yes, Annie, it is. I'm quite exhausted, and I'm sure Mr. Beaufort will understand if I decline his kind invitation." And if he doesn't, let him stew.

Annie looked hopefully at her. "Do you really mean that I can go to see my mother?"

"Yes, of course. I'm quite capable of existing for a while without a maid. I'm not entirely helpless."

"Oh, thank you, Miss Carberry. You'll never know how grateful I am."

"Go along now, Annie, and you can have the rest of the day. I'm sure Lady Eleanor will not mind, and if she does, then I'll say it's all my fault, which it is."

At a loss for words to express her gratitude, Annie hurried away, almost as if she was afraid Rosalind would change her mind. Rosalind smiled a little. It seemed that Annie was human, after all, with very human emotions. But then, didn't

every loving daughter worry about her mother? Rosalind
lowered her eyes. She was a loving daughter herself, but
she'd left home in such a way that distress was bound to have
been the result. True, she'd sent a note from Annapolis, but
it would have provided scant comfort. It was time to write
another letter, to let them know she'd arrived safely.

But as she went down to the floor below again, to the
drawing room, where she'd noticed a small writing desk the
evening before, she thought wryly that if things continued
to go the way they appeared to be going, she and the letter
would probably arrive back in Washington together.

She ignored Celia's portrait as she commenced the letter,
but she was conscious of its presence all the time. She didn't
tell her family of the disagreeable things that had happened
to her since her arrival in London; she just wrote about the
good things, such as they were. Well, she was in London,
she was staying at Southvale House, and both Lady Eleanor
and Katherine had been kind to her. It was also true that
Gerald Beaufort was coming to escort her over the town
today; there was no need to add that he was loathsome in
the extreme and that she wouldn't go out anywhere with him
if he were the last man on earth.

She'd just completed the letter when Richardson came to
inform her that Gerald had called and was waiting in the
entrance hall. She took her time about sanding, folding, and
sealing the letter, for it wouldn't do Gerald any harm to be
kept kicking his elegant heels for a while, and then, when
she was quite ready, she went down to speak to him.

He was standing by the fireplace, one hand resting on the
mantelpiece and one shining boot upon the polished fender.
He was looking into the flames and didn't at first hear her
approach. The firelight glowed on his face and burnished
his dark-chestnut hair to bright copper. He wore a mulberry
coat and cream corduroy breeches, and his waistcoat was
made of particularly fine silver brocade. A bunch of keys
was suspended from his fob, and a golden pin shone in the
neat folds of his starched neckcloth. His top hat, gloves, and

ebony-handled cane lay on the silver-topped table in the center of the hall.

She'd almost reached the bottom when he heard her. He turned quickly and came toward her. "Good morning, Miss Carberry," he said in a very agreeable tone.

"Good morning, Mr. Beaufort," she replied coolly.

The coolness wasn't lost upon him. "I see I have yet to redeem myself."

She didn't reply.

He exhaled softly. "Miss Carberry, I realize that I was a little rude yesterday—"

"A little rude? Sir, you were monumentally rude."

"Er, yes, I believe I was. Believe me, I'm truly sorry to have treated you so appallingly."

She eyed him suspiciously. "I find it hard to believe in such a complete *volte face*, Mr. Beaufort. You made your feelings toward me very plain indeed when we first met yesterday, and then, without warning, you are all sweetness and charm. Why?"

"Perhaps because I realized how wrong I was about you."

"Indeed?"

"Miss Carberry, I made a gross error of judgment, and I bitterly regret it now. If I could undo those minutes yesterday, I would, but the sin is committed now. All I can do is try to make amends, and I will do, if you will but give me the chance. It was Lady Eleanor's suggestion that I take you to see some of the sights of London this morning."

"I'm far too fatigued after my arduous journey to consider a carriage drive, sir," she replied firmly.

His hazel eyes were shrewd, and the faintest of smiles touched his lips, as if he knew it was just an excuse. "Well, I suppose that's understandable," he murmured. "Miss Carberry, fresh air is said to be a sovereign cure for fatigue, so perhaps a walk in the park would be beneficial?"

"Mr. Beaufort—"

"A short walk in the park, that's all I ask."

"*All* you ask? Sir, you're inviting me to ignore propriety."

"A maid can accompany us, indeed, I would expect such a precaution. Forgive me if I gave any impression to the contrary," he replied quickly.

But still she held her ground. "I would prefer not to, sir," she said candidly.

"Miss Carberry, have you declared war upon me? Can we not negotiate a little? Surely a cessation of hostilities is our joint goal?" He smiled winningly.

"What does it take to convince you, Mr. Beaufort?" she said coolly.

"I'm determined to get into your good books, Miss Carberry. Please take a walk with me."

She hesitated, for it was quite plain that he wasn't going to take no for an answer.

"Please," he pressed, smiling again. "I can instruct Richardson immediately concerning a maid to accompany us."

She gave in. "Very well, Mr. Beaufort. A short walk."

"Ten minutes only, I promise."

15

She went to put on her warm brown velvet cloak and her gypsy hat, for which she chose wide brown satin ribbons. Annie had already dressed her hair into a fine knot from which tumbled a number of thin ringlets, and all she had to do was recomb the framing of little soft curls around her face.

Taking a deep breath to prepare herself for what was bound to be a somewhat strained occasion, she left the pagoda room to go down to where he still awaited her. A maid waited discreetly by the door.

His glance swept over Rosalind as she descended the staircase, and he smiled. "How suitable for a walk, Miss Carberry," he said.

She gave him a smile of sorts, but didn't respond. He sounded so pleasant and charming that it was difficult to recall how he'd been the evening before, but she could and did recall that other Gerald Beaufort, and it was enough for her to use a very long spoon when supping with him.

He retrieved his top hat, gloves, and cane from the table, and then offered her his arm. "Shall we go?"

She rested her hand only lightly over his sleeve and didn't enjoy even that small contact. She didn't like him, she wished Lady Eleanor hadn't asked him to come here today, and she wished the walk was already over and done with.

Followed by the maid, they emerged from the grounds of Southvale House through the postern gate just below the terrace. She glanced up at the rotunda as they passed, and she saw that a maid was engaged in polishing the windows. The gardener she'd seen earlier was still busy, and there were two others and a boy with him now. All the potted plants had evidently been carried out to their allotted places, but now the path was being raked, nearby shrubs were being pruned, and the fallen leaves were being gathered so that the grass before Lord Southvale's residence was clear and green. They all paused as Rosalind and Gerald walked by, the maid still following, and after touching their hats respectfully, continued with their work. Rosalind could feel their speculative gazes following her, however, and wondered what the talk was among the servants. No doubt they were taken up with little else but the astonishing arrival of a prospective new Lady Southvale—an American one at that.

Gerald escorted her along the path and then north into the broad gravel walk she'd noticed earlier. It connected the Piccadilly end of the park with the Mall in the south, and was a place where a number of ladies and gentlemen strolled enjoying the sun. The buildings of Picadilly faced her, as did the northern boundary wall of the park, and in front of that she could see the shining stretch of water she'd observed from the rotunda while waiting for Katherine.

Gerald was determined to be agreeable and informative. "This is the Queen's Walk," he told her. "It's named after Queen Caroline, consort of King George the Second. It seems she wished to be able to walk privately in the park from St. James's Palace, and so this was originally not open to the public."

He smiled. "Royalty considers itself to be vastly superior to the rest of us, Miss Carberry, and Queen Caroline thought it a little more than most. We have to thank her for her interest in parks, however, for she was responsible for a great many improvements. Besides, it was her desire to exclude the rest of us that led to her early demise. There used to be a summer pavilion here, built solely for her, and she took to using it in all weathers. She went to it one particularly cold November day, sat there a little too long, and caught a severe chill, from which she died ten days later. Her private walk has been available to the rest of us for some time now, as are all the other royal parks.''

They strolled on, and the rectangular stretch of water ahead became easier to make out. Small boys were sailing toy boats on it, and there were some ducks.

Gerald saw her looking at it. ''It's the reservoir belonging to the Chelsea Water Works. There's always a great deal of water in the park, because the Tyburn stream passes beneath it. This reservoir, and another one in Hyde Park, close to Park Lane, provides water for Mayfair.'' He pointed his cane toward Piccadilly and the elegant streets to the north beyond it.

''Where do you live, Mr. Beaufort?'' she asked, remembering that the footman Richardson had sent looking for him yesterday had mentioned a house in Piccadilly.

Gerald pointed with his cane again. ''Do you see that house with the blue-painted dormer windows in the roof?''

''The narrow, four-story one?''

''Yes.''

''That is Maison Beaufort; at least, it will be for the next six months, after which my lease runs out and I'll be thrown out on the street.''

''Gambling debts?'' she asked directly.

His hazel eyes flickered over her. ''Yes, Miss Carberry, gambling debts. Do you disapprove?''

''I can't say I find it laudable, but it does seem to be the way of a great many gentlemen, including my own brother.''

He smiled a little wryly. ''But I'll warrant your brother hasn't plunged in quite as deep as me and that the duns aren't beginning to gather in packs at his door.''

''No, it hasn't come to that yet.''

''Don't believe it when you're told there aren't wolves in

Britain anymore, Miss Carberry, for there are, only now they're called debt-collectors. It's a novel experience being the hunted, not the hunter, and I've become quite cunning.''

"I'm sure you have. Is there nothing you can do to placate them?''

"I keep hoping to win vast sums at the green baize.''

"A downward spiral, sir.''

"So it increasingly seems. I'll have to find myself a rich bride, Miss Carberry.''

They reached the edge of the reservoir and paused for a moment to watch the toy boats bobbing on the water, then they turned to walk westward, parallel with Piccadilly, the noise of which was now tremendous. Hooves and wheels clattered, men shouted, dogs barked, stagecoach horns sounded, and various street calls rang out, from a woman selling lavender bags to a pieman recommending everyone to try his delicious hot wares.

Another path led southwest toward the center of the park, and Gerald led her along it, away from the bustle of the street. A light breeze had sprung up, rustling through the autumn leaves and toying with the hem of Rosalind's cloak. She could see the impressive facade of Buckingham House away to the south, and the rise of Constitution Hill, which got its name, so Gerald informed her, from the fact that King Charles the Second had enjoyed taking the air there after his triumphant return to his realm.

Gerald put himself out to be as attentive and interesting as he could, telling her everything he could think of about the park and its surroundings. But he didn't mention the mysterious mound in the middle, close to the two low hills. She could see the mound more clearly now and the rather eerie, delapidated building surmounting it.

At last her curiosity got the better of her. "What is that building over there, Mr. Beaufort?''

"King Charles the Second's icehouse, or what's left of it. Apparently he liked his wines and cordials cooled in the hot summer months, and so he had a very deep pit dug just there. The mound enclosed it, making sure it stayed cool, and the building kept it all safe from the weather. Ice was collected in the depths of winter, placed in the pit and covered with straw, bracken, sacking, and anything else they could think of. It all stayed cold enough for there to be ice constantly available for his royal table.''

"I do know what an icehouse is, sir, for we have them in America.''

He smiled apologetically. "Forgive me. I didn't mean to sound patronizing.''

"Could we go closer?''

"If you wish, but it isn't very pleasant. In fact, it's rather gloomy. It's falling apart, to be quite honest, and I doubt if it will remain there for much longer.''

They left the path and walked through the fallen leaves on the grass. The maid followed at a discreet distance.

"How does London compare with Washington, Miss Carberry?'' asked Gerald, ducking his head beneath a low-hanging branch.

"The cities are so very different that they can't really be compared.''

"Do you miss your home?''

"Yes.'' She looked away, for thinking about her home and family made her feel suddenly sad. She was only too conscious of how very far away they were right now.

The icehouse was indeed a gloomy place, and very cold indeed. It was built of stone, and was only one story high. Its windows were small and little more than slits, and its door hung open on only one ancient hinge.

The maid lingered a little way away as Rosalind stepped tentatively inside, shivering as the dank air folded over her. She could hear water dripping somewhere and see wisps of ancient straw lying on the uneven floor.

Gerald's shadow fell across the doorway behind her. "That's the pit over there, and it's very, very deep, so don't go near it.'' He pointed to one side.

She turned and saw the yawning black hole in the floor.

It was from there that the dripping sound was coming. She shuddered a little, for there was something almost ominous about the place. "I—I think I've seen enough," she said, turning and going out again.

He stood aside, grinning. "I did warn you that it wasn't exactly pleasant. But it is interesting. One can imagine the merry monarch demanding his chilled wine on a baking hot summer day."

"I'll warrant it wasn't as dismal in his day," she replied, glancing back through the doorway, glad to be out in the sunshine again.

"Probaby not." He smiled. "I'm sure crumbling icehouses aren't what you came all this way to see, are they? Visitors to London prefer the grand sights, like the Tower, St. Paul's cathedral—"

"I didn't come here to be a visitor, sir," she interrupted quietly.

His smile faded, and he became more serious. "No, I know you didn't. Again I must ask you to forgive me, for I didn't mean to suggest that your stay was going to be temporary."

"But nevertheless that's what you do think, isn't it?" she asked directly.

"I don't know what makes you think that, Miss Carberry."

"You make me think it, sir. On several occasions yesterday you seemed so certain that Philip wasn't going to marry again that I began to think you possessed some private information on the subject."

He looked uncomfortable. "Miss Carberry, I'm afraid I said a great many things yesterday, and I'm not proud of any of them."

"Nevertheless, you were certain on that, weren't you?"

He didn't respond.

"Mr. Beaufort, you said you wished to make amends for yesterday."

"Yes, but . . ."

"I'm asking you for your assistance. Why are you so certain that there isn't going to be a second Lady Southvale?"

His hazel eyes met hers. I don't want to upset you again, Miss Carberry.''

"I'll be more upset if you don't tell me.''

"Very well. Philip and my sister were very happy together, theirs was a love match of the very highest quality. He was grief-stricken when she, er, went away from him, and people began to wonder if he'd ever recover. Miss Carberry, I didn't see him at all when he returned from America, but I know that he suddenly had Celia's portrait put back in the drawing room. In my opinion, he came back to Southvale House and realized that his feelings for Celia were still too strong to be ended. He fell in love with you in Washington, where he was away from all the past, but back here in London, he was suddenly surrounded by memories again. He really did love her very much, Miss Carberry, and it was the sort of love that I don't think he can shake off. That's why I don't believe he'll marry again, for when it comes down to it, he can't contemplate replacing my sister with anyone else.''

Rosalind looked away, for it was only what she'd began to think herself.

"Miss Carberry,'' he went on gently, "I can't think of any other reason why he hasn't said anything to us about you.''

She raised her chin. "Are you saying you no longer believe I'm an adventuress who stole the signet ring?''

He looked embarrassed. "Yes, Miss Carberry, that is what I'm saying.''

"You're also saying you think that I'll soon be on my way home to Washington again.''

"He isn't going to marry you, Miss Carberry, for Celia still has first claim on his heart.''

She thought of the portrait, and memories of her dream slid over her, making her shiver again.

He saw the shiver and drew her away from the icehouse. "Let's leave this horrid place. My ten minutes is more than up, I fancy, and I don't wish to fatigue you anymore, so perhaps it would be best if we returned to the house.''

She nodded, and they began to walk eastward across the park toward Southvale House. The maid brought up the rear, still at a discreet distance.

As they walked, Gerald looked at Rosalind again. "Am I forgiven a little for yesterday?"

"A little."

"That will do to be going on with. May I call upon you again? Tomorrow, perhaps?"

"Mr. Beaufort, I'm sure Lady Eleanor won't expect you to give up another day on my account."

"Contrary to what you think, Miss Carberry, I'm quite happy to spend time with you. I know I didn't give any such impression yesterday, but my opinion of you has changed completely. I think you are a very agreeable and interesting person indeed, and the thought of enjoying your company again is very pleasing."

She looked at him in astonishment. "Do you also stand upon your head, sir?"

"It has been known," he murmured, smiling. "May I call upon you again?"

He made her feel uncomfortable, and she nodded, more because she wished to bring the subject to a close than because she wished to agree to his request. She still didn't like him, although she had to concede that he'd done everything possible to retract his rudeness of the day before.

As they walked into the entrance hall of the house, they found that Lady Eleanor had just that moment returned from her somewhat lengthy breakfast with her friends. She wore a mustard-colored gown and matching pelisse, and a black velvet hat trimmed with several aigrettes. She was standing by the fireplace, reading a note she'd found waiting on the table.

"Richardson?" she called suddenly. "Richardson, come here at once!"

The butler appeared at the double. "My lady?"

"When was this delivered?" She waved the note at him.

"I'm afraid I cannot say, Lady Eleanor. The new footman

has been attending to the door while I've been engaged with certain problems in the kitchens.''

"I'm not concerned with problems in the kitchens, sir," she replied tartly. "This note is from Lord Southvale, he's returning tomorrow evening at eight."

Rosalind's heart seemed to stop within her. Tomorrow? So that was when she'd know what her fate was to be. Was she still going to be the second Lady Southvale? Or would she soon be sailing back across the Atlantic to pick up the pieces of her former life, and to face the almost certain ruin of her character? Oh, the gossip in Washington would be tremendous. Rosalind Carberry had rejected a catch like George Whitby, had run away to England in pursuit of a dashing lord she hardly knew, and had, in turn, been rejected herself. What lady would have any name left after such a sequence of scandalous events?

Lady Eleanor looked at her, and not unkindly. "I'm sure everything is going to be satisfactorily resolved, my dear, and that the puzzle of Philip's reticence concerning you will be explained."

She turned and walked away across the hall to the staircase, and as she went slowly up toward her room, Gerald turned urgently to Rosalind.

"Miss Carberry, whatever happens tomorrow, you do know now that in me you have a friend, don't you?" he said.

"Mr. Beaufort, I hardly think—"

"I realize that we got off on an extremely bad foot, but I truly regret my behavior yesterday." His hazel eyes were serious. "If Philip should abandon his responsibilities to you, I . . ." He broke off, lowering his eyes for a moment. "Forgive me, I didn't mean to speak out of turn, it's just that I'm afraid you're going to be very badly hurt, and I want to help you if I possibly can."

Fresh disquiet rose within her. "Mr. Beaufort, you do know something you're not telling me, don't you?"

"No, Miss Carberry, I promise you I don't." He met her eyes again and didn't look away.

Her disquiet remained, but she had to accept his assurance.
"I—I think I'd like to go to my room now, Mr. Beaufort.
I really am tired after the journey."

"Yes, of course. Miss Carberry, with your permission I'd
still like to call upon you tomorrow. Philip won't be here
until the evening, so . . ."

"Call if you wish, Mr. Beaufort," she replied, wishing
he'd go away.

"Until then," he murmured, sketching her an elegant bow.

Richardson, who had been waiting a discreet distance
away, hastened to open the front doors for him, and a
moment later his carriage drove away across the courtyard.

The moment he'd gone, Gerald Beaufort slipped
completely from Rosalind's mind, for it was solely of Philip
that she thought. Oh, if only she knew what tomorrow's
reunion would be like . . . She wanted it to be joyous, but
a cold finger of doubt still touched her. Oh, how far away
tomorrow evening seemed, but she had no choice but to
endure the intervening hours as best she could.

Endeavoring to hide her inner uncertainty and fear, because
Richardson was still nearby, she went to the staircase,
gathering her skirts to go quickly up. Please let Philip still
love and want her. Please.

16

Time did indeed pass slowly until Philip's return. For the rest of that day Rosalind was in the company of both Lady Eleanor and Katherine, and in the evening there was an unexpected diversion from Annie.

Having given the maid the day off, Rosalind hadn't really expected to see her when she retired to her bed that night, but when she went up to the pagoda room after dinner, she found Annie waiting to attend her. Far from looking reassured after having seen her ailing mother, the maid had obviously been crying a great deal again, so much so that her eyes were very puffy and red.

Rosalind's own problems faded into the background for a while as she drew the unhappy maid to one of the fireside chairs and made her sit down. The she crouched before the chair, taking the maid's trembling hands. "Now, then, Annie, tell me what's happened. Is it still your mother?"

"Oh, Miss Carberry . . ." The maid couldn't say anything else, for the tears began anew.

Rosalind gave her her handkerchief and waited until she was a little more composed. "Can you tell me about it now?" she asked gently.

"The doctor's been to see her now, madam, and he said

that she has . . ." The maid hesitated. "It was a very long word, madam, and I can't remember it, but she has a very bad pain in her right side, and the doctor said there is a very bad abscess there, and that unless she has an operation, she'll die."

"I'm afraid he's right, Annie, for it's very serious indeed."

"But I can't afford an operation like that, madam. The doctor says it's very expensive, and very dangerous. If she has it, she'll be bedridden for a long time afterward, and certainly won't be able to take in laundry like she has been doing. She says such expense is out of the question for her, because she has all my little brothers and sisters to look after. I'm the oldest one, madam, and the only one in work, apart from Mam herself. Dad left just after my littlest sister was born, that's about five years ago now. We just can't afford the operation, Miss Carberry."

"Nor can you afford to leave things as they are," Rosalind said gently. "What will happen to your brothers and sisters if your mother dies? You can't be a lady's maid and look after them, and it's my guess that yours is the money that provides most. Am I right?"

"Yes, madam. My money's very important to Mam. That's why I have to keep my place, no matter what."

"Annie, your mother has to have the operation."

"But we can't afford it, madam."

"I'll give you whatever money you need."

The maid stared at her. "You'd do that? But I'm not even really your maid, madam."

"You're my maid at the moment, Annie, and as your mistress, I have a duty to look after you. I have a mother, too, and she matters very much to me. Besides, I'm sure I'm only doing what Lady Southvale would have done if she were still alive."

"Oh, no, madam, she wouldn't even have asked me what was wrong."

Rosalind stared at her. Celia Beaufort may not have been a saint, but surely she'd have had a little compassion for her maid's predicament.

Seeing her expression, Annie shook her head. "She wouldn't have cared, Miss Carberry, for she was unkind. She was alwyas saying she'd dismiss me without a reference. The only person in this house who mourned her was Lord Southvale himself, and he broke his heart over her. The rest of us didn't like her at all, and we're all glad about you, Miss Carberry, even Mr. Richardson. We only hope that everything's going to be all right and that you're going to marry his lordship."

Rosalind was a little startled to realize she had so much support belowstairs, especially when the butler had seemed so unfavorably disposed toward her the day before. "Annie, I'm flattered to know you all wish me well and rather surprised to find Mr. Richardson among my supporters."

"Mr. Richardson wasn't sure about you," admitted the maid, "for he said that it was very odd that his lordship had neglected to tell anyone about you, but when I told him this morning how you'd given me the rest of the day off just to see my mother, he said that that was the mark of a true lady. He said he was forced to change his view of you, for you were obviously worthy of his lordship."

"Thank you for telling me this, Annie. It's comforting to know you welcome me. I only wish . . ."

"Yes, madam?"

"I only wish I could be sure Lord Southvale himself is going to welcome me."

The maid stared at her. "But of course he will, madam. He gave you his ring."

"I no longer think it's as simple as that, Annie," replied Rosalind, getting to her feet again.

"Lord Southvale is the most honorable gentleman in London, madam, and if he asked you to be his bride, then he will marry you."

Rosalind wished she could have such simple faith. She looked at the maid again. "We mustn't forget the urgency of your mother's situation, Annie. Is it far to your home?"

"Southwark, madam, south of the river."

"Hire a hackney coach and take one of the footmen with you, for it isn't safe for a young woman to be alone in the dark. I will tell Lady Eleanor that I told you to do so. You must inform the doctor that I will meet any bills that arise where your mother is concerned, and that he's to proceed with the operation as quickly as he can."

"Yes, Miss Carberry." Annie got up and then hesitated, smiling shyly. "I don't know how to thank you, madam."

"You don't have to."

The maid bobbed a curtsy and then hastened out.

The next morning was wet, cold, and windy. Leaves were torn from the trees in Green Park, and the smoke from London's chimneys was snatched raggedly away by the blustering wind. Breakfast in the rotunda was out of the question on such a disagreeable autumn day, and so Rosalind ate inside with Katherine and Lady Eleanor, who both approved of her actions concerning Annie's mother. No one mentioned Philip's imminent return, and the omission was very loud indeed. Rosalind already had grave doubts about the outcome of meeting him again, and by the end of the meal she knew that his sister and great-aunt shared those doubts.

Gerald's arrival to escort her again came almost as a welcome diversion, for it served to take her mind off her unhappy situation. Annie accompanied them, because it was once again necessary to have a chaperone, especially for a lengthy drive across London. The maid was in a much lighter mood, for the doctor had performed the operation on her mother straightaway, and with complete success. A lengthy recuperation now lay ahead, but the immediate danger was past, and the change in the maid was very noticeable indeed.

No one could have been more attentive and considerate

than Gerald Beaufort. He showed Rosalind all the sights, from Greenwich and the Tower of London, to St. Paul's cathedral and the Palace of Westminster. He took her to Ranelagh Gardens and then showed her the prime minister's residence in Downing Street, Almack's assembly rooms in King Street, and the Italian Opera House, where Signora Segati was soon to appear. They had luncheon at Grillion's Hotel in Albemarle Street and then joined the afternoon display in Hyde Park's Rotten Row, where he pointed out numerous famous people, from politicians and admirals to artistocrats and actresses.

Gerald was kindness personified, and so very conscious of her every need that she began to feel a little uncomfortable, for it was plain that from disliking her intensely in the beginning, he now viewed her very warmly indeed. Far too warmly. He held her hand for a little too long when she alighted from the carriage, and he smiled a little too frequently whenever she spoke. There was an admiring and inviting look in his hazel eyes and something that told her she had to tread very carefully, for fear of seeming to encourage him in any way.

But at last the afternoon began to draw to a close, and it was time to go back to Southvale House. The moment of Philip's return was very near now, and with each passing moment her feeling of deep apprehension increased. The streetlamps were being lit as the carriage bowled along St. James's Place and into the courtyard of the house, and as it drew to a standstill, Gerald leaned forward to take her hand suddenly.

"'Miss Carberry, I would like to be present when Philip arrives," he said.

"I—I can hardly prevent you, sir," she replied, gently withdrawing her hand.

"If you would prefer me not to, I will do whatever you wish, but I do feel that you may be glad of as many friends as possible."

He did know something, there was no mistaking the

certainty in his eyes. He knew that Philip was going to reject her. Her pulse quickened, and the awful feeling of vulnerability that had first come over her in Falmouth now returned with swinging force.

Gerald alighted, turning to assist Annie down first and then Rosalind. His fingers closed a little too warmly over hers, and again she began to pull her hand away, but he tightened his grip a little, drawing her resisting fingers to his lips. "I will call again within the hour, Miss Carberry."

"As you wish, Mr. Beaufort," she replied, almost snatching her hand free.

Followed by Annie, she hurried up the steps to the doors, which opened before her as a vigilant Richardson attended smoothly to his duties.

In the warmth and brightness of the entrance hall, Rosalind turned to the maid. "Mr. Beaufort knows something, doesn't he?"

"Well, he *does* seem to," agreed the maid.

"He's far too certain that things aren't going to go my way tonight, and he was equally as certain yesterday as well."

"But what can he possibly know, Miss Carberry?"

"I wish I knew."

"Things are going to go well for you tonight, madam," reassured the maid. "I just know they are."

"Well, we'll soon see, will we not?" murmured Rosalind, moving toward the staircase.

Annie exchanged an unhappy look with the butler and then followed her new mistress up to the pagoda room.

Now that darkness had fallen, the autumn wind seemed to howl even more around the eaves. It drew down the chimney, making the fire flare in the hearth, and the slight draft swayed the candles glowing in the porcelain pagodas.

It was nearly eight o'clock, the time appointed for Philip's return, and Rosalind sat before the dressing table while Annie put the final touches to her hair, which was pinned up in the Grecian style that became her so well. She wore a long-sleeved gray velvet gown, high-waisted with a low, scooped neckline, and with it an amethyst pendant and matching earrings. The amethysts winked and flashed in the light of the candlestick placed on the dressing table next to the mirror.

Putting the last pin in place, Annie went, as previously agreed to, keep watch from a window overlooking the courtyard, so that she could tell Rosalind the moment Philip's traveling carriage arrived. Everyone else, including Gerald, was already waiting in the drawing room, and they had been expecting Rosalind to join them for some time now, but she couldn't bring herself to sit in awful anticipation with them. No, she intended to let Philip arrive and speak to them first, before she summoned the courage to face him, or them.

Only a few minutes had passed before Annie came hurrying back. "He's here, madam!"

Rosalind's heart almost stopped and then began to race unbearably. Annie brought the same knotted shawl she'd carried at the Washington ball, and she rose to her feet, feeling almost sick with anxiety. Please let the outcome of this be good . . .

She went slowly to the head of the staircase and paused there, leaning over the marble balustrade to look down past the gilded Chinese lanterns toward the entrance hall, two floors below.

Richardson was already waiting and must have heard Philip's steps, for he went quickly to the doors, flinging them open. "Welcome home again, my lord."

Rosalind waited breathlessly for her first glimpse of the man she loved and had come so very far to see, but as he stepped inside, all she saw was his heavy gray Polish greatcoat and his top hat.

Richardson waited attentively. "I trust you had a good journey, my lord?"

"The five miles from Greys isn't exactly arduous,

Richardson," replied Philip, turning for the butler to help him with his coat.

"Greys, my lord? But—"

"I needed to think, and it's as good a place as any." Philip teased off his black leather gloves and gave them to the butler. "Is all well here?"

"Yes, my lord, except—"

"If there are any problems, I'll make myself available a little later."

"Yes, my lord, but I think you should know—"

"I said later," interrupted Philip firmly, removing his top hat and pushing it into the other's hands.

Richardson fell silent.

Philip glanced around the entrance hall, and Rosalind could see him properly at last. He wore a dark-purple coat and tight-fitting cream breeches, and there was a large diamond pin in his complicated neckcloth. He was a little thinner than she remembered, and his face looked pale and drawn, but his eyes were still an incredible blue. He ran his fingers briefly through his tangle of coal-black hair, glancing at the butler.

"Are my sister and great-aunt in?"

"Yes, my lord, they are waiting in the drawing room. Mr. Beaufort is also here."

"Dammit, what the devil's he here for?"

"I believe he wishes to see you, my lord. We've all been most concerned about you."

"I'm a big boy now, Richardson, and well able to take care of myself," Philip replied dryly.

"Yes, my lord."

"I'll go to them, then."

"My lord." The butler bowed and withdrew.

Philip paused for a moment, toying with his cuff, then he turned abruptly to come lightly up the first flight of the staircase.

Rosalind drew hastily back from the balustrade. She heard

him pause again on the floor below, then he pushed open the doors of the drawing room and went in.

She took a deep breath in an endeavor to compose herself, then she went very slowly down to the next floor.

17

Rosalind could hear the voices in the drawing room before she could see through the doorway.

Lady Eleanor was the first to speak. "Ah, there you are at long last, Philip."

"Good evening, Great-aunt Eleanor. Katherine. Gerald."

Gerald murmured the usual reply, but Katherine gave a glad cry, and Rosalind heard the rustle of her turquoise taffeta skirts as she ran to greet her brother. "Philip! Wherever have you been?"

"Greys."

Katherine gave a disbelieving gasp. "But I sent a message there, and Mrs. Simmons—"

"I instructed her to say I wasn't there."

"But why? Philip, what has been going on?"

Lady Eleanor made a concurring sound. "Yes, Philip, what has been going on?"

"I had something of immense importance on my mind."

"So important that you couldn't be bothered with the courtesy and consideration we usually merit?" inquired the old lady a little tartly, for she was very displeased with her great-nephew for behaving in such a cavalier fashion.

Philip knew he deserved to be on the receiving end of this

displeasure. "You must forgive me, Great-aunt, but I really did need to be on my own for a while."

Rosalind had reached the floor below now, and she moved hesitantly toward the drawing-room doors. She could see the little group quite clearly, and Celia's portrait, watching over them as if paying attention to every word they uttered. Rosalind paused just beyond the pool of light by the doorway, where the softer glow of the Chinese lanterns by the staircase lost the battle to the brightness of the chandeliers in the drawing room.

Lady Eleanor was surveying her great-nephew rather severely. "Yes, Philip, I'm quite sure you do have something to think deeply about, for matters of marriage aren't to be lightly brushed aside."

Philip was very still for a moment. "Matters of marriage?" he replied slowly.

"Yes. Come, now, sir, let's not beat about the bush, for all of us here present know what's behind all this."

"You do?" His glance moved briefly to Celia's portrait and then away again.

"Yes, and we rather feel we're due an explanation. It really isn't good enough for you to leave us in the dark like this. It's all come as a dreadful shock, you know."

He gave a dry laugh. "Oh, I know that, Great-aunt, I know it only too well."

"Don't you think you should have given us some intimation of what had happened? As it was, we simply had the lady in question turn up at the door."

He stiffened, his piercing blue eyes resting urgently on the old lady. "She's here already?"

"Yes, of course she is. How else do you imagine we've found out about it?"

"I just presumed . . ." Philip looked at Gerald for a moment. "I presumed wrongly, it seems," he finished, his voice little above a murmur.

Gerald met his gaze and then looked at the fire.

Katherine, who still stood next to her brother, having hurried to hug him on his arrival, now looked at him, a little perplexed. "Philip, you don't seem exactly pleased to know she's here in London."

He smiled a little wryly. "Are you pleased, Katherine?" he asked softly.

"Of course I am, for she's everything that is pleasing and kind." Katherine couldn't hide her indignation. "Why do you think I'd be *dis*pleased?"

"I may have been blind in the past, Katherine, but I've worked a few things out for myself since then."

She stared at him. "What on earth are you talking about?"

"I'm talking about you and . . ." He suddenly broke off, whirling about as if some sixth sense told him Rosalind was there. He stared at her as if he'd seen a ghost, and his face, already pale, became more pale still. "What in God's name are you doing here?" he breathed.

Rosalind's heart faltered and she couldn't reply. There was no welcome in his eyes and no kindness in his voice.

He came slowly toward her, halting a few feet away. "You shouldn't have come, Rosalind, for there's nothing here for you, and the sooner you go back where you belong, the better."

Had he physically struck her, she wouldn't have known more pain than she did in those few shattering seconds. She'd prayed for a happy reunion, and she'd feared a rejection, but she'd never dreamed that that rejection could be as cruel as this. "Philip, I . . ."

"We need to talk in private, madam," he interrupted, glancing back at the astonished trio behind him. "I'll await you in the library." He strode past her, walking along the landing to another doorway on the other side of the staircase. The room beyond seemed to be in darkness, but he went inside and closed the door behind him.

Lady Eleanor and Katherine seemed to be rooted to the spot with shock and dismay, for nothing could have been more embarrassing than what had just happened.

It was Gerald who seemed to recover first. He came quickly over to Rosalind, closing the drawing-room doors so that he and she were alone outside. He took her hands. "Don't forget that I'm here if you need me," he said quickly.

She hardly heard him, for she was still too overcome with misery at the way Philip had behaved.

"Look at me, Miss Carberry."

His urgency penetrated and she did as he bade, but her green eyes were accusing. "You know why he's changed toward me, don't you?"

"I'll be here if you need me," he said again.

"It's Philip I need, sir," she replied, noting that he'd evaded her question.

"But Philip now appears to be beyond your reach, Miss Carberry, whereas I am most definitely here."

It was a blatant declaration, and her breath caught in astonishment. "What are you saying?" she whispered.

"I think my meaning is clear enough," he said, holding her gaze. "Philip may no longer want you, Miss Carberry, but I most definitely do."

With a gasp, she pulled away from him, gathering her skirts to hurry toward the library door.

As she went inside, she saw Philip holding a candle to the fire. Shielding the new flame with his hand, he went to a table, lighting a candelabrum that stood there. The new light wavered softly over bookshevles and damson velvet curtains, and she was aware of the comfortable smell of leather from the armchair and the bindings of the books.

He faced her. "Why did you come here, Rosalind?"

"I mistakenly believed you loved me, sir," she replied, her voice shaking a little.

A nerve flickered at his temple and he looked away for a moment. "You left Washington before you were due to, I take it?"

"That much is obvious, sir."

"If you'd done as we'd agreed, you'd have received a letter

from me. I wrote it in time to catch the *Queen of Falmouth* packet.''

"The *Queen of Falmouth* is believed to have been lost at sea, and anyway I'd probably left before she was due to arrive. What did you say in the letter, Philip?''

He drew a long breath, returning to the fireplace and leaning a hand on the mantelpiece, his back toward her. "It wasn't a very explanatory letter; in fact, it was little more than a note. I wrote in complete detail a few days ago."

It was like talking to a stranger. This wasn't the Philip de Grey who'd laid such sweet siege to her in Washington; it was someone she didn't know at all.

He glanced at her again. "Why did you leave early?"

"Several reasons. My mother became unwell and my father decided that the wedding would have to be put off well beyond Christmas, and then the political situation worsened so much that it really did seem as if war would break out at any moment. I decided I couldn't risk the possibility of being parted from you for what might prove to be a very long time, so I left secretly and alone to join you here."

He turned quickly. "You're here alone?"

"Yes."

"Oh, Rosalind . . ."

"I realize now that I'm a complete gull, but I had no idea that you'd changed so much toward me. After all, when last we spoke, you did beg me to join you, and I was rather under the impression that you wished me to be your wife. Evidently I was wrong."

He met her gaze for a moment and then turned back to the fire. "This is the very last thing I wished to have happen, Rosalind. Please believe me."

"I no longer know what to believe, sir," she replied. "You did ask me to marry you, didn't you? I begin to wonder if I dreamed it all."

"You have my ring to prove it wasn't a dream," he said, glancing at her left hand.

"Well, that can obviously soon be rectified." She removed

the ring and placed it on the table by the candelabrum.

He gazed at the gleaming gold and said nothing.

"Philip, aren't you at least going to give me an explanation?" she asked.

He nodded. "Yes, I'll tell you what's happened, but before I do, I want you to know that I meant everything I said to you in Washington."

"Yes, I think you probably did, Philip, but that was before you came back here to her, isn't it?" She spoke quietly, but every word was clear. This was all because of Celia, so why not be open about it?

He looked at her. "Do you mean Celia?"

"Has there ever really been anyone else?"

"Oh, yes, Rosalind, there's you."

Tears pricked her eyes. "But you don't want me, do you, Philip? You've made that very plain, just as you've made it equally plain that you still love Celia."

His blue eyes searched her face. "And how have I done that?" he asked softly.

"You've moved her portrait back to the drawing room."

He pressed his lips together almost ruefully. "Yes, I suppose I did do that."

"And you didn't tell anyone here of my existence, did you? Would you mind telling me why?"

"To protect you."

She stared at him. "Protect me?"

"Maybe it was a foolish notion on my part, for the whole of Washington knows about our betrothal, but I still thought it better for you if I said nothing on this side of the Atlantic. My second letter explains it all . . ."

"Which is more than you're doing right now, my lord," she interrupted softly. "I fail to see how you can be protecting me at all, because no matter what, sir, my ruin is now assured. I've thrown caution to the winds, and with it I cast aside my reputation."

He put a hand out toward her and then let it fall away again. "I'm sorry, Rosalind, but I really have no choice. You see, on my return to London, I discovered that Celia is still alive and that she'll soon be returning to me.''

Thunderstruck, Rosalind could only gaze at him. Whatever else she'd expected, it hadn't been this. She felt the color drain from her cheeks and had to reach out to the table to steady herself.

"That's why I said there was nothing here for you," he went on, "and why I think it would be best if you returned to Washington, where you belong. My first thought was of shielding you as much as possible from the shame that's bound to attach to you because of this, and all I could think of as preventing you from leaving Washington."

Tears shone in her eyes. "Nothing can shield me, my lord, for I've committed the sin of running away after a married man." She gave a slightly bitter laugh. "John was right, wasn't he? He said that you weren't over your wife, but he didn't know how very accurate he was."

"Please, Rosalind . . ."

"I'm sorry to have embarrassed you by coming here, Lord Southvale, and will remove myself as soon as possible."

"Rosalind . . ."

"Will tomorrow be soon enough, or would you prefer me to go tonight?"

"You know there's no need to leave tonight," he said quietly.

"Do I? I'm afraid I no longer know anything at all where you're concerned, my lord. Good night." Striving to cling to her dignity and composure, she turned and walked out of the room, closing the door behind her.

For a moment he didn't move, but then he went to the table to pick up the signet ring. His fingers closed convulsively over it, and with a stifled cry he turned to hurl it into the heart of the fire.

Rosalind was blinded by tears as she ran toward the staircase, intending to go directly to her room, but she found Gerald barring her way.

He caught her by the arm. "What's happened, Rosalind?"

He used her first name, but she barely noticed it. "Please, let me go . . ."

"I need to know what he said, Rosalind." He glanced toward the drawing-room doors, knowing that Lady Eleanor and Katherine might emerge at any moment.

Even in her distraught state, Rosalind at last realized that he'd again addressed her by her first name. She stiffened, fighting back the tears in order to look coldly at him. "I gave you no leave to be so informal with me, sir."

"Rosalind, just tell me what's been said."

"Unhand me."

Her green eyes were chilly and imperious, and he released her.

"Mr. Beaufort, I rather suspect that you already know what he told me. Your sister is still alive and is about to come back to him."

He didn't deny it. "What does he intend to do?"

"Discard me. What else?" Her gaze was frosty. "So much for your professed wish to be my friend, sirrah."

"I do, believe me. In fact, you must know by now that I wish to be far more than just a friend to you."

"A friend would have told me the truth, Mr. Beaufort, and would have spared me the humiliation of tonight. But you let me go on hoping for the best, didn't you? I'll never forgive you, sir, and as for ever needing you, well, I wouldn't turn to you if you were the last man on earth."

"You're very upset at the moment, I realize that, but—"

She cut him off in midsentence by hurrying away up the staircase. The tears were stinging her eyes again and all she wanted was to hide away in the sanctuary of the pagoda room.

Annie was still there and turned in dismay when she saw how upset her new mistress was. "Oh, Miss Carberry . . ."

Rosalind closed the door and then leaned wretchedly back against it. "Well, at least the truth is known at last," she said quietly.

"Truth, madam?"

"I'm not going to be the next Lady Southvale, because there is still a holder of the title."

Annie stared at her. "Are—are you saying that Lady Southvale is still alive, madam?"

"Yes, I am. And not only is she still alive, but she's on the point of returning to her husband."

"Oh, no, it can't be so."

"It is, and what's more, Mr. Beaufort knew about it. First impressions are nearly always right, aren't they? I knew him for a toad during the first few seconds, and now he's proved himself to be just that."

"Miss Carberry, has Lord Southvale said he's taking her back?"

"Yes."

"But he loves you, madam!"

Rosalind smiled wryly. "No, Annie, he doesn't love me. I was but a fleeting fancy, a diversion to take his mind off his sadness. He still loves her and has told me that there's nothing here for me."

"He really doesn't love you?" Annie's eyes were urgent.

"No. She's the one he's always loved."

The maid lowered her eyes. "I wish he wanted to be rid of her," she said quietly.

"I'm afraid it's me he wishes to be rid of, so the sooner I leave, the better for all concerned." Rosalind looked quickly at the maid. "I shall still honor my promise to you concerning your mother's medical expenses."

Annie lowered her eyes, blinking back sudden tears. In the brief time she'd known Rosalind, she'd come to hold her in very high regard indeed.

Taking a deep breath, Rosalind went to sit at the dressing table. "I'll leave as soon as a chaise can be secured for me. Will you tell Richardson in the morning?"

"A chaise, madam? Isn't his lordship going to provide you with his traveling carriage?"

"I haven't asked him, and I don't intend to. I prefer to hire a chaise."

"Yes, miss. I'll tell Mr. Richardson."

"I'll take the chaise to Falmouth and then obtain passage on the first available packet."

"I'm so very, very sorry, Miss Carberry. If only his lordship still loved you."

"Well, he doesn't, Annie, there's no mistake about that. His first reaction on seeing me was the true one: he told me there was nothing here for me, and that the sooner I returned to America, the better. Those aren't the words of a man in love with me, are they?"

"No, madam, they're not."

"Unpin my hair, Annie, for the sooner I change and retire to my bed, the sooner I bring this dreadful day to an end."

"Yes, madam."

18

But Rosalind wasn't able to retire to her bed for a little while, because Lady Eleanor and Katherine came to see her just as she was about to take her wrap off. At first she didn't want to face them, but at last gave in and told Annie to open the door.

Katherine hurried straight to her. "Oh, this is all quite dreadful!"

"I take it you know what's happened?"

"Yes, the *chienne* has returned out of nowhere."

Lady Eleanor went to sit on one of the fireside chairs. "*Chienne*, indeed," she murmured.

Rosalind glanced at her in surprise. So the old lady was yet another who didn't admire Celia.

Lady Eleanor made herself comfortable and then looked at Rosalind. "I can't tell you how much I regret all this, Miss Carberry, for although you've only been with us for a very short while, I've nevertheless formed a very favorable opinion of you."

"Thank you, Lady Eleanor."

"I cannot believe that Philip is still so blind as to love that odious creature and can only presume that he's taking her back out of duty."

Rosalind shook her head. "He still loves her, my lady,

there's no question of it." She hesitated. "Is he still here?"

"No, my dear, he chose to avoid the inevitable quizzing he'd received from Katherine and me, and he's removed to his club for the rest of the evening. He refused to answer any questions before he left, so we're rather hoping that you may be able to shed a little light on everything."

"Me? I don't know anything," replied Rosalind.

"Did he tell you where Celia has been for the past year or more?"

"No, and I didn't ask him. All I know is that she's still alive and that he expects her to be with him again soon."

Katherine sat dejectedly on the edge of the bed. "I can't believe all this is happening," she murmured. "I really hoped that you were going to become my sister-in-law, Rosalind." She smiled sadly. "I know it may seem pointless now, but I really would like to call you Rosalind. Do you mind?"

"No, of course not."

"And you must call me Katherine. Oh, this is all so unfair! Celia's coming back to make us all miserable again, and Philip's turning his back on the one he should marry."

"He still loves Celia," Rosalind reminded her quietly.

"I don't even think she was faithful to him," cried Katherine, getting up from the bed.

Lady Eleanor looked severely at her. "That's quite enough, Katherine."

"But—"

"I said that's quite enough," repeated the old lady sternly. "Whatever you may think, you must not say it. Your brother's wife is returning to him, and since he evidently still loves her, then you must hold your tongue."

Annie kept her gaze fixed firmly on the floor, but Rosalind looked quickly from the old lady to Katherine, remembering Mrs. Penruthin and the mention of a certain Dom Rodrigo de Freire.

Katherine was close to tears of frustration and anger. "I don't owe that creature any favors."

"No, you don't," agreed the old lady, "for she was very

unkind to you, but if you set out to try to alienate her from Philip, I fear that in the end you will be the one who is alienated from him. He wants her back, child, and no matter how much we may chafe against it, there's nothing we can do. Miss Carberry is the one who has to pay the highest price, for she has forfeited her reputation. She is innocent, the victim of circumstance, but I'm sure that Washington gossip is as odiously unfair as in any other city. Am I right, Miss Carberry?''

"I fear you are, Lady Eleanor."

"When do you intend to leave us?"

"As soon as a chaise can be secured. I've told Annie to instruct Richardson in the morning."

"A chaise? But, my dear—"

"I don't want the use of Philip's carriage, Lady Eleanor," Rosalind interrupted firmly.

For a moment the old lady seemed about to try to persuade her, but then decided against it. She rose slowly to her feet. "I fear I must retire to my bed, for I have one of my headaches. There'll be another change in the weather before morning. Thunder, if I'm not mistaken. Come along, Katherine. Good night, Miss Carberry."

"Good night, Lady Eleanor."

"I'm deeply sorry that all this has occurred, for I would have been very glad to welcome you permanently to the family. You do know that, don't you?"

"Yes, I do." Rosalind smiled at her.

As the old lady went out, Katherine suddenly hurried to Rosalind, flinging her arms around her neck, and hugging her. "I wish you weren't going, I wish so many things, and none of them is going to come true. I was unhappy in love, so I know how desperately miserable you must be now." Then, stifling a sob, she hurried out after her great-aunt.

Annie closed the door quietly behind them and then came to turn back the bedclothes for Rosalind. "Is there anything else you wish me to do, madam?"

"No, that will be all, Annie. Oh, you may extinguish the candles."

"Very well, madam."

A moment later the candles were all out, leaving curls of smoke to drift in the firelit room. Rosalind took off her wrap and then climbed into the bed. She lay staring up at the Oriental canopy, conscious of a feeling of great emptiness. Her worst fears had been realized—oh, how they'd been realized—and now all thought of happiness had been cruelly wrenched away. She still loved Philip de Grey with all her heart, but that love was no longer returned, if, indeed, it ever had been. Had he loved her in Washington? Or had it just been an illusion, not only to her, but to Philip himself? He had gazed upon her and had been momentarily distracted, that was all it now seemed to have been. How she wished she hadn't so blindly followed the dictates of her heart, but had listened to John instead. But fools rush in where angels fear to tread, and now she was paying the price of that foolishness.

Sleep didn't come, and the minutes passed interminably slowly as she lay gazing at the canopy. A church clock struck midnight, and then one o'clock, and still sleep eluded her. She heard a carriage in St. James's Place and realized that it was turning into the courtyard. It must be Philip returning from his club.

She tried to close her eyes, but it was impossible to contemplate sleep. Flinging back the bedclothes, she got up to go to the window, drawing back the curtains and then folding the shutters.

The wind had subsided outside, and all was very still, so still that a mist had risen in the park, caused, no doubt, by the unseen waters of the Tyburn. A movement on the terrace below caught her eye, and she looked down to see Philip walking toward the little rotunda. He went inside and closed the door behind him.

She hesitated and then impulsively turned to put on her

wrap. She had to speak to him, for there was still so very much to be said between them.

The night air was cold and damp as she emerged onto the terrace, and she could smell the autumn leaves in the park. The mist swirled eerily between the trees, but was as yet lower than the terrace. She shivered as she went quickly toward the rotunda, for her wrap was only flimsy.

She opened the door and saw him lounging wearily back on one of the chairs. He leapt to his feet as she appeared. "Rosalind?"

"I saw you from my window. I must speak to you again, Philip."

"No good will come of it."

"Maybe not, but I had to come down here to see you. I'm leaving as soon as a chaise can be secured, hopefully some time tomorrow, I mean, today . . ."

"A chaise? Rosalind, I insist that you use my carriage."

"No, Philip, I won't be beholden to you."

"Beholden?" He gave an ironic laugh. "That is surely the last thing you will ever be."

"Maybe so, but it's how I feel. It's better if I hire a chaise."

"My carriage will be at your disposal if you change your mind," he said quietly, his glance moving over her and coming to rest on her golden hair as it spilled loosely over her shoulders.

"Did you ever really love me, Philip?" she asked.

"Yes. You know that without asking."

"Do I?"

The faintest of smiles played on his lips. "You should do," he said softly.

"Then you should know that I still love you," she said with painful honesty.

"Don't say that, Rosalind. Please don't say that."

"But I do still love you, and I can't stop just because of what's happened. I came all the way just to be with you, to give myself to you . . ."

He came closer, putting a finger swiftly to her lips to stop her words. "Do you think I'm made of stone, Rosalind? Do you think I'm finding it easy to turn away from you?" His hand fell away again.

"I don't know, Philip. All I know is that Celia has come back, and there's no longer any room for me in your heart."

"She's my wife, and she's been ill. Now she needs me and I have a duty toward her."

"Ill?"

He turned away, going to a window and looking out over the misty park. "It seems she was saved from the shipwreck by a passing Portuguese vessel. She was barely alive and had struck her head, with the consequence that she'd lost her memory. She didn't recover it until a few months ago, when she struck her head again in a riding accident. The family who have been looking after her all this time wrote to me, and the letter was waiting here when I returned from Washington."

So Katherine had been right, the change in him had been due to something in the accumulated mail. "Where has Celia been all this time?"

"Somewhere just outside Lisbon."

Rosalind stared at him. Mrs. Penruthin's voice suddenly echoed in her head: ". . . A Portuguese nobleman by the name of Dom Rodrigo de Freire. He'd been in England for some three months, visiting London after serving with the Duke of Wellington in Spain. He was very handsome and dashing, and very wealthy, for he had fine estates outside Lisbon. His ship set sail for Portugal on the same tide that hers left for Ireland . . ." Surely it was all too great a coincidence? "Philip, what is the name of the family she's been with?"

"Name? I don't know, the signature was illegible. I think someone called Dom João wrote it, yes, that's it, Dom João, but as to the surname, well, it was impossible to read. It's strange actually, because the rest of the letter was very clearly written indeed."

Rosalind fell silent, but her every instinct told her that Celia hadn't lost her memory at all and hadn't even been on the ship that had gone down. She'd been in Portugal for the past year, with her lover, Dom Rodrigo. The affair had probably run its course and now she wanted to come back.

Philip turned to face her again. "The letter said she'd soon be leaving for England and that I was to expect her at any time. I knew that it was out of the question for me to continue our betrothal, Rosalind, so I wrote a brief note, asking you not to leave Washington, and I sent a man to Falmouth to catch the *Queen of Falmouth* before she sailed. I didn't want to give you up, but I had no choice, for I was no longer free to offer you anything."

"You—you didn't want to give me up?"

His eyes were very blue, even in the virtual darkness of the rotunda. "No."

"Philip, do you still love Celia?"

He hesitated and then shook his head. "No."

She stared at him. "Do you love me?"

"My darling Rosalind, I love you so much that it hurts to be so close without taking you in my arms. Somehow I'm going to have to exist without you, and it's a prospect so bleak that I don't know how I will endure."

A limitless joy swept weakeningly through her. "Oh, Philip, I think I can bear anything if I know you still love me."

He closed his eyes for a long moment. "I have no right to love you now, Rosalind."

She went to him, linking her arms around his neck and kissing him on the lips. For the space of a heartbeat he tried to resist, but then he swept her into his arms, almost lifting her from the floor as he crushed her close. His fingers curled richly in her hair and he could feel the wild beating of her heart. The love and desire she'd aroused from the first moment cried bitterly through him again now. He'd never love anyone as he loved her, but he had to give her up.

Slowly he relinquished his hold, putting his hands up to disengage her arms. "This is wrong, Rosalind . . ."

"I know," she whispered, tears wet on her cheeks.

He cupped her face in his hands. "You're so very lovely," he said softly. "You will fill my nights and my days, and you always will. That's why I had to move Celia's portrait back into the drawing room. I tried to remember her, but all I could see was you."

Rosalind closed her eyes, more tears wending their way down her cheeks.

He rested his forehead against hers, his thumbs caressing gently. "I know I deluded myself about Celia, for she wasn't the paragon I chose to convince myself she was. I'd even begun to suspect her of having lovers, but I didn't want to believe it of her, and when she died, I felt guilty for having doubted her. I think I was out of love with her before she left for Ireland that last time, but I was conscience-stricken because I'd secretly thought ill of her. Rosalind, any feelings I may once have had for her are now quite cold, and if I could with honor take you as my wife, believe me I would, for you mean everything to me. But she is still Lady Southvale, and I owe her a duty. You do understand that, don't you?"

She nodded, unable to speak.

He brushed his lips tenderly over hers, tasting her tears. "Go now, my love, before I give in and beg you to stay with me."

A sob caught in her throat as she drew back from him, then she turned and hurried out into the night. The mist had crept up over the terrace now, lying in a swirling, silver-gray carpet across her path. It recoiled as she went by, and then folded silently over again, hiding the telltale marks of her passing.

19

Dawn was a long time coming, and when it did, the mist swiftly dispersed, leaving the air oddly and unpleasantly humid after the wind of the day before. Low clouds dulled the sky, and sound seemed to travel a long way. Rosalind knew that Lady Eleanor had been right: there would soon be a thunderstorm.

When Annie at last brought the morning tea, she told Rosalind that it was proving very difficult to hire a chaise, because word was out of a famous prizefight taking place that afternoon on Crawley Down, on the Brighton Road, south of London. Such was the interest in the fight, which had had to be arranged at the last moment because such encounters were illegal, and their whereabouts were always kept secret for fear of intervention and arrests by the law, that every available chaise had been snapped up, and so had every livery horse, for it seemed that most of London's gentlemen would be sallying forth to watch the celebrated encounter. Nothing could be promised until late that evening, and there was nothing for it but to wait until then.

Rosalind hadn't brought all that much luggage with her, so there was no need for Annie to begin packing until the evening. Rosalind could therefore choose to wear anything from her somewhat limited wardrobe, and she decided upon the primrose sprigged muslin gown that had the matching pelisse and wide-brimmed hat. She'd worn this outfit to drive into London, so why not wear it again to drive out?

She maintained an admirable composure as she sat before the dressing table for Annie to comb and pin her hair. Memories of what had happened in the rotunda during the night seemed to be all around her still: she could feel Philip's arms around her, taste his lips, and hear the loving words he'd said. Leaving him would be the most difficult and heartbreaking thing she'd ever had to do, but she knew she had to go, for she had no right to love another woman's husband, and that husband had no right to turn his back on his wife.

There was a discreet tap at the door and Annie hastened to open it. It was Philip. He was dressed very formally in a black corded silk coat and white silk breeches. A tricorn was tucked under his arm, and he wore silk stockings and highly polished black pumps. He glanced pointedly at Annie, who took the hint and withdrew, then he looked at Rosalind.

"I was evidently seen arriving last night, for word has been sent this morning summoning me immediately to the Foreign Office."

"About St. Petersburg?"

"Yes." He put the tricorn down, smiling a little self-consciously. "One is required to wear the correct togs for such high places."

"You look very elegant."

"Rosalind, Richardson tells me that you're still insisting on a chaise."

"Yes."

"He also tells me that because of the prizefight, there apparently isn't a chaise to be had until late this evening."

"Yes, but I should still be able to travel a little way out of London."

"Then you'll still be here when I return from Whitehall." He paused. "I don't want to keep this appointment, Rosalind, but I have to. When I come back, I'd like to spend a little more time with you before you leave."

She rose slowly from the dressing table. "Is that wise?"

"No, but I'd still like to be with you."

"And I with you," she said softly.

He hesitated, and she went to him, slipping her arms around his waist and holding him tightly. He returned the embrace, his cheek resting against her hair. For a long moment they just stood together, then he pulled away, turning to pick up his tricorn before leaving the room.

Her lips trembled, and she swallowed, determined not to succumb to the tears that seemed ever-present.

She didn't know Katherine had come in until she spoke. "Are you all right, Rosalind?"

Rosalind turned quickly, giving a brave smile. "Yes, of course I am."

"It's just that I saw Philip leaving this room a moment or so ago, and now I've found you almost in tears . . ." Katherine's peach-and-white-striped gown whispered softly as she came farther into the room, closing the door behind her. "What did he say to you?"

"Just that he'd like to see me when he returns from Whitehall." Rosalind hesitated, but then couldn't help telling her what else had happened. "He still loves me, Katherine, he told me so last night in the rotunda." She explained everything.

Katherine's eyes widened. "Celia's been in Portugal?" she said at last.

"So it seems."

"With a lost memory?" Katherine's lips twitched disbelievingly. "Do you think it's true?"

"Not after what I was told by Mrs. Penruthin."

"What were you told?" Katherine asked attentively, sitting down on a fireside chair. "I do hope it blackens Celia's character beyond redemption."

"It blackens her character, all right, but I'm afraid it's

guesswork.'' She explained about Dom Rodrigo and the rides on the moors above Falmouth. ''He has estates near Lisbon,'' she finished on a meaningful note.

Katherine stared at her. ''Are you quite sure?''

''It's what Mrs. Penruthin said. She was convinced they were lovers, but couldn't prove it.'' Rosalind went to the window, looking up at the gray skies. A wind was beginning to stir through the park, and leaves fluttered through the air. There weren't many people strolling on the Queen's Walk, for it wasn't the right kind of day. Her glance came to rest upon a solitary woman wearing a rich dark-blue velvet cloak. She was slender and seemed rather nervous, but Rosalind couldn't see her face because the cloak's hood was fully raised. She was walking south toward the Mall, and she glanced now and then toward the house, but her face remained invisible. A low rumble of thunder sounded in the distance.

Katherine came to stand next to her. ''My great-aunt was right, we are going to have thunder. She's seldom wrong, she can always tell by her headaches.''

''How is she this morning?''

''Still in her bed. She insists she still has the headache, but I think it's as much because she's upset about you. She really has taken to you, you know. Just as I have.'' Katherine smiled, linking her arm. ''I really can't believe fate is being so cruel. You and Philip love each other, but are going to have to part because of a vixen like Celia. And now it seems he'd begun to doubt her even before she was supposed to have died, and that he'd probably fallen out of love with her before then, too.''

Rosalind felt the salt tears pricking her eyes and hurriedly blinked them away.

Katherine squeezed her arm. ''I feel so wretched for you, I just wish there was something I could say or do to help.''

''There isn't anything.''

''Oh, if only we could prove she'd been up to no good

during this past year—and before, come to that."

"She may have been the perfect wife all along," reminded Rosalind.

"Pigs will fly over Mayfair first," replied Katherine succinctly.

Another growl of thunder spread across the distant sky outside, and they both looked out again. Rosalind noticed the cloaked woman once more. She was walking north toward Piccadilly now and still seemed to glance occasionally toward the house.

Katherine looked at Rosalind suddenly. "Was Philip quite certain that that letter was written by a Dom João?"

"Yes, I think so."

"What if he was wrong? What if it was Dom Rodrigo?"

"It would be very convenient if it was, but I don't think Dom Rodrigo or Celia would write a letter that so closely incriminates them. The letter states that Celia had lost her memory and that she'd only remembered everything after a riding accident. Dom Rodrigo was with her in Falmouth, and quite definitely knew who she was then. He'd have had to lose his memory too not to have been able to identify her all this time."

"That's very true, but I'd still like to see the letter. Philip seldom destroys his letters, not even those that displease him, so I'm pretty certain this particular one will still be somewhere in the house. In his study, probably. I think I'll go and have a look." Without waiting for Rosalind to reply, she gathered her skirts and hurried away.

Rosalind sighed, for it was hardly likely that anything to her advantage would result from the letter. She looked out at the windswept park again. A flash of lightning lit up the sky, and as another roll of thunder followed, the first scattering of raindrops struck the windowpane.

The wolman in the dark-blue velvet cloak was standing motionless on the Queen's Walk, staring toward the house. Her hood was still raised and her face in shadow, but there was no mistaking her interest in Southvale House. Another jagged flash of lightning illuminated the clouds, closely followed by a clap of thunder so loud that it made Rosalind start.

A stronger gust of wind blew across the park, suddenly flinging back the woman's hood, and Rosalind saw with a gasp that it was Celia. Rosalind's heart missed a beat, for it was almost as if the drawing-room portrait had come to life; she was seeing Celia Beaufort against a thundery sky . . .

More rain dashed against the glass. Celia quickly pulled up her hood and began to hurry away directly across the park, following a much smaller path than the broad gravel walk.

Rosalind didn't hesitate, but went swiftly to the wardrobe to take out her own cloak. Putting it quickly around her shoulders, she left the room and ran down through the house toward the terrace. The wind caught the cloak, billowing it wildly as she hastened toward the little flight of steps at the far end of the terrace.

Rain was falling heavily now, but she hardly noticed as she went down toward the postern gate and then out into the park. There she paused for a moment, gazing toward the middle of the park, in the direction she'd last seen Celia. She caught a brief glimpse of the dark-blue cloak, then it vanished between the autumn trees somewhere near the icehouse.

Gathering her own already-wet cloak, Rosalind hurried after it. A vivid flash of lightning dazzled her, and her heart pounded fearfully as a tremendous clap of thunder shook the very ground. The rain had become a downpour, and she could feel the cold seeping through to her shoulders.

A double flash of lightning split the sky, followed by an explosion of thunder that reverberated between the trees. She'd thought it was already raining as heavily as it could, but the downpour became a veritable cloudburst, and she could barely see where she was going. She could just make out the silhouette of the icehouse, and made her way toward it, pushing thankfully inside.

The rain rattled on the ruin's crumbling roof, and the drawing wind stirred the dank air. Water still dripped into the pit, but more persistently now, as the storm water seeped swiftly through the holes in the roof.

There was a sudden movement in the shadows, and with a sharp gasp Rosalind turned quickly, her eyes widening.

Celia stood there, her lilac gaze full of malevolence. "Well, I had hoped to avoid the woman who so vainly presumed she could usurp my place, but it seems we're destined to confront each other, after all, Miss Carberry."

20

Rosalind stared at her, caught off-guard not only by the other's unexpected presence in the icehouse, but also at being addressed by name.

Celia smiled a little. She was as lovely in the flesh as she was in the portrait, and there was such an air of sweetness about her that it was impossible to believe she wasn't what she appeared to be. Outside there was another flash of lightning and a roll of thunder that seemed to growl for a long time across the leaden skies. There was no lessening of the cloudburst, which pounded into puddles by the doorway and rattled on the roof as if it would come directly in to where the two women stood facing each other.

Another faint smile curved Celia's lips. "Have you nothing to say, Miss Carberry?"

"How do you know who I am?"

"Oh, you fit your description, my dear, and I did see you looking out the window. I didn't think you'd seen me, however, but you did, and here you are."

"How long have you been in London?"

"A week or more."

Rosalind's lips parted in astonishment. "And you haven't come to the house?"

"To be with those two tabbies while Philip was away? Hardly, my dear."

Rosalind studied her, wondering what was going on in her mind. "He came back yesterday," she said, "but then you already know that, don't you? Your brother has been keeping you informed about everything."

Celia smiled again. "Yes, he has."

"Have you been staying at his house in Piccadilly?"

"Yes. I see no point in denying it. If Philip asks me the same questions, I shall say that Gerald said nothing because I specifically asked him not to, and that I stayed away from the house both until he was there and out of consideration for your unhappy predicament, my dear. He'll think me so exquisitely sensitive and considerate to put your feelings before my own, and my hold over him will consequently be stronger than ever."

"Are you quite sure of that?"

"Oh, yes, my dear, for I know how to captivate him, and I have the marriage bed in which to do it. My poor Miss Carberry, you'll never share his marriage bed now, will you?"

The wind sucked through the icehouse, breathing coldly over Rosalind. She shivered a little, conscious of the wet cloak clinging against her. Lightning flashed again, followed by a rumble of thunder that seemed perceptibly farther away.

Celia was still intent upon Rosalind. "I suppose I can imagine how you felt when you learned that I was still alive."

Rosalind lowered her glance. Yes, my dear Celia, but can you also imagine how Philip felt? He's no longer the adoring husband you left behind; it's me he loves now.

Celia was provoked by her enigmatic silence. "How very galling it must have been for you, my dear, to have come all this way to become the second Lady Southvale and to have achieved nothing but your own ruin. How will you face Washington society after this? The gossip will be rife, will it not? And all because I have returned from the dead."

"No, Lady Southvale, it's all because you've come back

from Portugal,'' replied Rosalind quietly, her voice barely audible above the roar of the rain.

Celia's lilac eyes flashed. "I was hardly on vacation there, Miss Carberry.''

"Weren't you? What happened, my lady? Did Dom Rodrigo tire of you, or was it the other way around?''

It was a calculated stab in the dark, but it found a target, for Celia couldn't quite disguise the guilty start that resulted from the careful choice of words. Then a mask descended over her beautiful face. "I don't know what you're talking about, Miss Carberry. Who is this Dom Rodrigo you mention?''

Celia gave herself away with that single query, although she didn't yet know it. Rosalind's breath escaped on a long slow sigh of satisfaction, for suddenly it was quite clear that her suspicions about the real events of the past year were correct. She smiled at Celia. "Come, now, Lady Southvale, how can you possibly not remember Dom Rodrigo? He was the gentleman you shared such intimate moments with at Falmouth and with whom you've been near Lisbon for the past year or more.''

Celia's eyes were veiled. "I don't know a Dom Rodrigo,'' she said again, but there was disquiet in her glance.

Another draft of cold, damp air made Rosalind shiver, and she glanced up for a moment as the rain lashed the roof. Water was dripping in many places now, and she could hear it falling into the nearby pit, the sounds echoing chillingly through the shadows. She returned her attention fully to Celia. "Why bother to deny him, my lady? You were never on that Irish ship, were you? For the past twelve months and more you've been living with him on his estates near Lisbon. The shipwreck cannot have come into you original plans, but it must have come as a welcome bonus, for it made it so easy for you to claim to have been saved and then to return to the life you'd so casually set aside for your own selfish pleasures.''

"What a wildly improbable story, Miss Carberry.''

"But fairly close to the mark, I think."

"You'd have to prove it, of course." Celia smiled. "How very tiresome for you, my dear, to have guessed the truth, but not to be able to do anything about it."

Rosalind drew a long breath. "So, you admit it?"

"I see little point in denying it any longer, since you've, er, rumbled me, as they say. I will deny it all to anyone else, of course, and will say that you're just lying about me out of jealous spite." Celia's eyes were a vivid lilac as another flash of lightning lit the skies outside. "You're right about the shipwreck; it was indeed a bonus, but I'd intended to be lost overboard anyway. I didn't go on the ship, but my baggage did, and so did a local Falmouth girl I'd paid handsomely for her services. She was dressed in my clothes, with a veiled hat to conceal her face, and she entered the cabin that was reserved for me. Then she left in her own clothes just before the ship sailed. When the ship arrived in Ireland, my absence would have been put down to my having been lost overboard during the crossing."

"Didn't you care how much grief and pain you caused? Philip suffered tortures of grief over you, and I've no doubt that your family in Ireland thought themselves bereaved as well."

Celia shrugged. "I was infatuated with Rodrigo and wanted to be with him."

"Not infatuated enough to simply inform Philip that you were leaving him for your lover. No, you laid your plans very carefully, always intending to return if things didn't go as you wished."

"I don't believe in burning my bridges, Miss Carberry," replied the other smoothly.

"Oh, I've come to realize that, my lady."

"Yes, you probably have, but Philip still intends to take me back, and there's absolutely nothing you can do about it."

"Why did you decide to return?"

"Because Rodrigo and I had grown tired of each other, and because I'd begun to yearn for the delights of London.

Lisbon is a very dull place, Miss Carberry, and can't hold a candle to this city. When I told Rodrigo I wished to return, he was only too willing to be of assistance. It was his letter that Philip received, for he said that it would be more convincing if the letter was in a hand Philip didn't know. I'm sure he was right, for it added weight to the tale of lost memory and caring strangers in a foreign land." The lilac eyes sharpened and rested warningly on Rosalind. "Don't think of trying to prove anything against me through Rodrigo, Miss Carberry, for he will deny everything. He doesn't want me back, and I don't wish to go to him, so we aren't going to oblige your aspirations by betraying ourselves."

Rosalind looked at her with loathing. "Philip really doesn't deserve a creature like you," she said quietly, her words clear in a momentary break in the rain.

"I'm still his wife, my dear, and he's such an honorable man that he won't hesitate to welcome me back into his arms. I don't really care what his feelings are toward you; they are of no consequence. His duty lies with me, and it won't be long before I've won him back entirely. As I said before, I have the marriage bed in which to convince him, and I intend to share it with him tonight." Celia gave a taunting smile. "I'm given to understand that you'll have left London by then, Miss Carberry, but if you haven't, I shall still lay claim to my husband, make no mistake of that. I'll tell him that I thought you'd gone and that I wouldn't have dreamed of causing you further humiliation by actually arriving in the house before you'd gone. He'll believe me, my dear, for I'm an excellent actress. Take my advice, be out of Southvale House before seven o'clock this evening, for that is when I intend to return to my husband's loving arms."

"Is that an ultimatum?"

"Take it as you please, but if you're still there, be prepared to see how effortlessly I can win him back. You'll cease to matter within a few minutes of my return, Miss Carberry."

Rosalind held her gaze. "And how long will it be before you're bored again, my lady? How long will it be before

Dom Rodrigo enters your life? Maybe I should stay here in London, to be on hand when next you betray your marriage vows. You've covered your tracks very well this time, but maybe next time you'll slip up. He's worth fighting for, Lady Southvale, and it seems to me that I shouldn't give up hope of eventually winning him.'' Rosalind hardly knew the thought was in her head, and she certainly didn't know if she meant it, but it was worth saying simply for the effect it produced.

"Don't stay here if you wish to retain a shred of your reputation, my dear," Celia hissed. "Society's sympathy will be with me, and I won't lose an opportunity to stain your name or compromise you if I possibly can." Then she smiled. "But I doubt very much if you'll carry out your threat, you're far too noble and proper for that.''

"Can you be sure?''

"I think so. You're already preparing to bow gracefully out of Philip's life, and that proves to me that you're a virtuous and high-principled young lady. You're a credit to your parents and to your nation, Miss Carberry, and I shall always be eternally grateful to both." Celia adjusted her hood, for the rain had dwindled away now, although the storm itself still growled across the sky nearby. "Good-bye, my dear, I trust you suffer the tortures of *mal de mer* all the way home, as well as the tortures of knowing I'm in Philip's loving arms. Remember now, be gone from that house by seven this evening, or I will crush your heart completely."

Holding her hood in place, Celia slipped out of the icehouse. For a moment Rosalind didn't follow, but then she left as well. She paused outside, for she could see Celia hurrying away toward Piccadilly and the northern gates of the park.

The noise of the busy London thoroughfare carried an air that seemed to have been washed clean by the storm. A sea of umbrellas bobbed along the pavements, and the clink of pattens was clearly audible. Stagecoaches, wagons, and other vehicles splashed along through deep puddles, and another distant roll of thunder proclaimed the storm's retreat to the south of the river.

Celia went out through the park gates and made her way across the street toward Gerald's house, which Rosalind could see quite well from the icehouse mound. As Celia went u p
the steps to the door, it opened, and Gerald himself emerged, looking very stylish in a fawn coat and top hat, cream breeches, and peacock-colored waistcoat. He paused on seeing his sister, and they exchanged a few brief, rather angry-seeming words; then he hurried on down to the curricle that was waiting at the curb, unnoticed previously because Rosalind's attention had been solely upon Celia. He drove off eastward along Piccadilly, cracking the whip to bring the two horses up to a smart pace, and Celia went into the house.

Rosalind turned away, retracing her steps across the wet grass toward Southvale House. So much she'd guessed about Celia was now confirmed, but at the same time it was impossible to prove. Oh, if only there was some way of giving Philip undeniable evidence of his wife's infidelities and heartless scheming, but Celia Beaufort was a clever woman and had covered her tracks very carefully indeed.

The sound of a whip cracking made Rosalind stop, for it sounded like Gerald's, and it came from St. James's Place. She moved to stand close to a nearby tree, watching the house, for if Gerald had called, she had no desire to return. She was wet and cold and in fear of catching a chill, but the thought of another confrontation with him was even more disagreeable. As she watched, he suddenly appeared on the terrace, going to stand by the summerhouse, his gaze scanning the park. She moved hastily behind the tree, remaining absolutely still. Celia had obviously told him of the encounter in the icehouse, and it seemed that he must have called to explain his part. The fact that he was looking at the park meant that it was she, Rosalind, that he'd come to see. Surely he didn't still intend to press his attentions upon her? Was he so insensitive? Or was it simply that he was so arrogantly sure of himself that he was convinced she'd be persuaded in the end? She could only conclude that it was a little of both, for he hadn't hesitated the day before to tell her that he wished to be more than just her friend, and he'd said it when she'd just emerged in tears from facing Philip in the library. Celia's brother was as loathsome and unpleasant as Celia herself.

At last he went away from the terrace, and a few minutes later she heard his curricle driving into St. James's Place. She hurried gladly toward the house, for she was now very cold and uncomfortable indeed.

Richardson was in the entrance hall as she made her way toward the staircase. His rather surprised glance flickered over her wet, somewhat bedraggled appearance, but he bowed politely, holding out a small silver tray upon which lay a folded sheet of paper.

"Mr. Beaufort called, madam, and he waited for a while, but then had to leave. He asked me to give you this."

She took it reluctantly and read. "Miss Carberry. Under the circumstances, I'm sure you will agree that we should talk. I will call again in one hour's time, when I trust you will receive me and allow me to explain. Gerald Beaufort." Well, he trusted in vain, for she had no intention of receiving him or of allowing him to explain anything to her.

The butler was still waiting, and she nodded at him. "That will be all, Richardson. I shall not be sending a reply."

"Madam." He bowed and began to withdraw, but then paused, clearing his throat a little deferentially. "Begging your pardon, madam . . ."

"Yes?"

"I wish to say how very sorry I am that you will be leaving us."

"Thank you very much, Richardson."

"Madam." He bowed again and then moved away in the direction of the kitchens.

Rosalind began to go up the staircase, but as she did so,

Katherine hurried down excitedly. She seemed to be almost bursting to say something, and her peach-and-white-striped gown fluttered.

"Oh, there you are at last, Rosalind. I seem to have been waiting an age for you to come back. Wherever have you been?" She halted, looking in astonishment at Rosalind's damp cloak and rainswept hair.

"I've been in the park," replied Rosalind.

"In this weather? Oh, no matter, for I have something very important to tell you."

"And I have something important to tell you," Rosalind said quietly. "Celia is in London; I've just spoken to her."

Katherine stared at her. "She's actually here?"

"Yes. I saw her from my bedroom window just after you'd gone to look for the letter, and I followed her across the park to the icehouse, where we'd both coincidentally decided to shelter from the worst of the storm. She intends to come here at seven this evening, whether I am still here or not. She's so very confident, Katherine, and I believe she could lie her way out of any situation."

Katherine recovered a little from the shock of learning that Celia was so near, and she suddenly seized Rosalind's hands reassuringly. "She can't lie her way out of everything, and I promise you that she's about to be undone."

"What do you mean?"

"The Portuguese letter was from Dom Rodrigo de Freire. Annie recognized his writing. There were other letters, you see, written before Celia left that last time for Falmouth, and they prove that she was being unfaithful to Philip. There's real proof, Rosalind, so you and Philip may not have to part, after all!"

21

⚜

"Do you really mean it?" whispered Rosalind, hardly daring to hope.

Katherine didn't reply immediately, for her great-aunt's maid hurried down past them, vanishing in the direction of the kitchen. "We can't talk here, let's go to your room. Annie's there and can help you with your clothes while we talk. But, yes, I do mean it, I mean every word." Taking Rosalind's hand, she ushered her up the staircase.

Annie hurried anxiously forward the moment they entered the pagoda room. "Oh, Miss Carberry, I'd have said something about the letters if I'd realized, but you said his lordship didn't love you anymore, so I didn't think the letters would serve any purpose for you. I didn't know she was still alive, truly I didn't, for the letters don't say anything about going to Portugal, just about meeting in Falmouth. You do believe me, don't you?"

The maid was almost in tears, and Rosalind put a reassuring hand on her arm. "Yes, of course I believe you, Annie."

"I thought that his lordship was still in love with her and that he wanted her back again. I'd have said about the letters straightaway if I'd known he loved you and wanted you to be his wife."

Katherine went to sit down by the fire. "You help Miss Carberry with her wet things, Annie, and I'll explain what's happened since I found the letter in the library."

"Yes, Miss Katherine." The maid began to remove Rosalind's cloak and then unhook the gown.

Katherine looked at Rosalind. "I brought the letter back here to show you, but you'd vanished. Annie was here, however, and happened to see me reading it. To my utter astonishment, she said that the writing belonged to Dom Rodrigo de Freire, even though it purports to be from a Dom João Something-or-other. It's very distinctive writing, look." She took the now crumpled letter from her sleeve and held it out to Rosalind.

The writing sloped noticeably and the loops were so long that they touched the lines above and below. It was very clear and legible, except for the signature, which was quite obviously a disguised scrawl.

Katherine watched her. "You can see why Annie recognized it, can't you?"

"Yes, but I don't know how she knew it was from him."

"Ah, well, let Annie explain that."

The maid helped Rosalind to put on a dry wrap and then led her to the dressing table to begin unpinning her wet hair. "It was like this, Miss Carberry, Lady Southvale was always a very difficult mistress, never satisfied or pleased with anything I did, and as I've told you before, she liked to threaten me with dismissal without a reference. What I didn't tell you is that on the day she left for Falmouth that last time, she really did dismiss me. I think now that she must have thought I'd found out about her affair with Dom Rodrigo and wanted me safely out of the way. I hadn't found out, though; in fact, I didn't know anything about it at all. Anyway, that last morning she told me that she no longer required my services, and that when she left, she expected me to immediately remove myself from Greys, which is where the family was in residence at the time. No one thought anything of her leaving without me, for she seldom took me on her visits to Ireland. I think now it was because she often met her lovers on the way.''

Rosalind looked quickly at her. ''Do go on, Annie.''

''And so I decided not to say anything to anyone about having been dismissed. Lady Southvale hadn't had time to tell anyone, because she was already very late leaving on account of the carriage needing a last-minute repair, so I knew that I'd be safe from discovery until she returned. She was due to be away for two months or more, and that meant two months' money for Mam. You do understand, don't you, madam?''

Rosalind nodded. ''Yes, Annie, I understand.''

''Well, only a few days after she'd left for Falmouth, his lordship suddenly decided to have Greys redecorated throughout, starting with her ladyship's rooms. He, Miss Katherine, and Lady Eleanor removed here to Southvale House, and most of the servants were to follow a few days later, when the redecorating was under way. I happened to be in her ladyship's dressing room when the workmen had to move a very large wardrobe in order to paper the wall behind it. There was a little hiding place there, with a bundle of letters tied up with red ribbon. I took it without the men even seeing, and went to my own room to see what the letters were.''

Annie blushed a little. ''I know I shouldn't have read them, Miss Carberry, but I'm afraid I did. They began from when her ladyship had been in Brighton a few months earlier, and the last one was dated only a few days before she left. They were quite clearly the letters of a lover, and there was no mistaking that she'd been committing adultery with him. They didn't say about running away to Portugal together, though, just that they'd spend time together in Falmouth. I decided that I could use the letters to make her ladyship give me the reference I needed to find another position, and so I hid them, ready for when she came back. I meant to tell her I'd give them to his lordship unless she wrote out properly for me.''

Annie lowered her eyes ashamedly. "It would have been blackmail if I'd done it, I know that, but I was desperate for myself and for my family. Anyway, as it happened, I didn't have to use them, because news reached London shortly afterward that she'd been lost in the shipwreck, and I didn't think any more about the letters. I haven't said any of this to anyone until today, Miss Carberry, for I knew that I shouldn't really be here anymore. Lady Southvale dismissed me, and Lord Southvale doesn't know she did."

Katherine smiled sympathetically at her. "Don't worry, Annie, for both Miss Carberry and I can quite understand the awful dilemma you were in."

"But she's coming back now, Miss Katherine," said the maid.

"And if the letters are still safe where you hid them, they're going to be used against her. If it doesn't work, you may be sure that both I and my great-aunt will gladly give you the reference you need."

"Thank you, Miss Katherine, but I hope they do work, for I'd like it more than anything if Miss Carberry became Lady Southvale." Annie smiled shyly at Rosalind. "I know you have a maid of your own, madam, and that when she's better, she'll come to you again, but I'll always be more than willing to attend you."

"Thank you, Annie, I'm very flattered, but I fear we're all counting our chickens. We haven't recovered the letters yet, and we don't know what Lord Southvale's reaction to them will be."

Katherine looked at Rosalind. "But we do know that he still loves you, and I'm sure that if the letters give him any just cause to set Celia aside, he will do so."

Rosalind smiled a little, but still didn't dare hope too much. She caught Annie's eyes in the mirror. "Where did you hide the letters? Are they really safe?"

"Oh, they're safe, madam, for I put them somewhere no one ever goes now. I hid them behind a loose board above the door of the little tree house by the lake at Greys."

Katherine suddenly rose to her feet, her face changing. "Oh Annie, I just didn't think when you told me earlier," she said in utter dismay.

Annie lowered the comb she held. "Think about what, Miss Katherine?"

"About the tree house." Katherine's eyes fled to Rosalind. "Philip was there a few days ago, I don't know exactly when, and was horrified to see how dilapidated it had become. He's ordered it to be completely repaired, taken apart if necessary, and the workmen are starting today! I heard him telling Richardson only this morning after breakfast, and it slipped my mind completely until now. We have to go there immediately if we're to save the letters. It may be too late already!"

Rosalind was appalled. "Oh, no . . ."

"I'll have Richardson order the carriage now," declared Katherine firmly, but as she moved toward the door, there was a knock and the butler himself came in to tell her that her great-aunt wished her to read to her.

Katherine was in a quandary, turning helplessly to Rosalind. "What shall I do? I know my great-aunt welcomes Celia's return as little as I do, but I don't want to raise her hopes too much over the letters."

"Stay here and read to her, Katherine," Rosalind said quickly. "I'll go to Greys with Annie."

"Are you sure?"

"Quite sure."

Katherine looked at Richardson, who was still waiting in the doorway. "Have the traveling carriage brought around and tell the coachman he'll be driving to Greys."

"Yes, Miss Katherine."

"And tell him it's urgent, so he's not to dawdle all the way."

"Yes, Miss Katherine." He bowed and quickly withdrew.

Katherine smiled ruefully at Rosalind. "I wish I was coming with you, but I really don't want to upset my great-aunt any more than she is already. It would be dreadful if

I told her all about the letters and then nothing came of it.''

"It's best if you just go and read to her, and then, hopefully, we can tell her some good news later,'' replied Rosalind.

Katherine came to give her an encouraging hug. "You're going to be my sister-in-law, after all, Rosalind, I just know it! You and Philip are perfect for each other, and you'll make him far happier than Celia ever did." Then she hurried away in the direction of her great-aunt's room.

As the door closed behind her, Annie hurried to the wardrobe to select something suitable for the journey to Greys. She took down the apricot wool gown and a gray velvet pelisse that Rosalind hadn't worn since arriving in England. With them she brought a gray velvet jockey bonnet, around the crown of which she quickly tied a long apricot gauze scarf that would hang down almost to Rosalind's hem at the back.

Her hair had been brushed and was now almost dry, so the maid quickly pinned it into a simple knot, and a few minutes later both maid and mistress were ready and waiting only for the arrival of the carriage.

Annie waited in a room overlooking the courtyard, and the moment she saw the vehicle appear, she hurried in to tell Rosalind.

They both left the pagoda room and walked quickly to the head of the staircase. Rosalind glanced uneasily at the maid. "What if we're too late? What if the workmen have already begun their tasks? If they are going to practically take the tree house to pieces . . ."

"Don't think about it, Miss Carberry, just tell yourself that we are going to find Lady Southvale's letters where I hid them at Greys, and that they'll make it possible for you to marry his lordship, after all."

As they reached the landing by the drawing room, Rosalind suddenly froze, for Gerald Beaufort was standing waiting at the foot of the staircase. She'd forgotten his intention to call on her again. But why hadn't Richardson announced him? Then another thought struck her: how much of her conversation with Annie had he overheard?

He gave no sign of having overheard anything, but gave a brief, rather tentative smile as he looked up the staircase toward her. "Good morning, Miss Carberry."

"Sir."

"I trust the presence of the traveling carriage doesn't signify your imminent departure for Falmouth?"

"No, sir, it doesn't." The question reassured her, for it meant that he couldn't have heard anything.

"I'm glad, for I have much I wish to say to you."

She looked coolly at him. "You can't have anything to say that I would wish to hear, sir," she said, going on down toward him.

"Did you receive my note?"

"Yes."

"Then, after what happened in the park earlier, you must know why I wish to speak to you."

"All I know is that I think you are a wretch of the first order, sir, in every way as odious as your sister, and I have no wish to speak to you at all. If your sole purpose in coming here is to attempt to reason with me, you're wasting your time."

He barred her way, just as he had the evening before. "I need to speak to you, Rosalind."

Her green eyes were haughty. "Don't presume, sir, for I still do not give you leave to address me familiarly."

His glance moved briefly to Annie and then back to Rosalind. "At least hear me out in private. Is it so much to ask?"

"Under the circumstances, yes, it is. You knew your sister was still alive; indeed, she's been staying beneath your very roof, and yet you let me go on thinking—"

"Celia didn't want anyone to know about her return until she'd been able to see Philip, and she specifically asked me to say nothing to anyone. I gave her my promise, and now beg you to understand my predicament."

"I understand well enough, sir. I understand that you've behaved very basely and forwardly toward me, and that as a consequence I dislike you intensely. I don't wish to have anything more to do with you, sir, and I most certainly don't regard you as anything remotely approaching a friend."

But I could be so much more than just a friend to you, for it's possible for me to save you from the humiliation and scandal of having to return to Washington. I can offer you marriage, and my name."

She stared at him, unable to believe her ears. "You can't possibly be serious," she breathed incredulously.

"Never more serious in my life."

"Your audacity amazes me, sir, and I promise you that the thought of marrying you fills me with revulsion. I prefer to take my chance with Washington gossip than sully my family and honor by turning to a toad like you."

The mask of friendliness slipped away from his hazel eyes, and his lips became thin with anger. "I would advise you not to speak to me like that, madam," he said softly.

"Ah, the real Gerald Beaufort appears once more! I'm amazed you managed to dissemble for so long."

"You'll soon be very sorry for spurning my advances, Miss Carberry."

"Are you threatening me?"

"I promise you that I'll exact full revenge for this, madam. In the end you'll wish you'd never come to London."

"Please go," she said, a little frightened by the controlled force she'd unleashed in him.

A slight movement to her right behind her suddenly caught her eye, and he turned with a quick, jovial smile. "Ah, Richardson, just the man!"

The butler came slowly forward, his eyes moving uneasily from Gerald to Rosalind, and then back to Rosalind again. "I didn't know you'd called, Mr. Beaufort."

"I have something I wish you to do for me."

Rosalind stared at Gerald, for the change in his manner was formidable. The vitriolic man of a few moments before was now a pleasant, completely charming gentleman.

Richardson bowed politely to him. "Yes, Mr. Beaufort?"

"I've decided to attend the prizefight on Crawley Down and will drive there immediately. Will you send someone around to my address to inform them where I'll be?"

"Yes, sir."

Gerald's hazel eyes flickered toward Rosalind again, and the faintest of smiles twisted his sensuous lips. "Good-bye, Miss Carberry, I trust you enjoy a fair journey back to America."

She didn't reply and exhaled with relief as he walked away.

Richardson turned to her. "Is everything all right, madam?"

"Yes. Thank you."

"When I first came into the hall, I thought Mr. Beaufort was, er, threatenng you, Miss Carberry."

"I believe it's over and done with now, thank you."

"If you're sure, madam?"

"Quite sure. We'll leave for Greys now."

"Madam." He hurried to open the door for her, and as they went out, they were just in time to see Gerald tooling his curricle across the courtyard at almost breakneck speed. His face was set with anger and he didn't spare the whip.

They set off in the carriage only a moment later, and as the elegant buildings of St. James's Place slid past, Rosalind leaned her head back against the blue velvet upholstery. Oh, how she hoped the letters were still safe, and how she prayed that they would lead to Philip's complete rejection of his spiteful, unfaithful wife.

22

It seemed an age before the carriage reached Tottenham Court Road and began the long uphill climb northward toward Hampstead Heath. The city of London soon began to fade away behind as the road passed through rolling, wooded countryside where meadows, orchards, and pastures were interspersed with cottages and farms. Hawthorn hedges lined the wayside, their branches heavy with fruit, and all around there was the russet, gold, and crimson glory of high autumn. There was no sign of the storm now; the sky was clear and blue and the sun shone brightly down.

The steady climb took its toll of the horses, and it was a long while before the spa of Hampstead appeared at the foot of the heath ahead. The little town had developed on swampy, sloping ground around the springs that had eventually made it fashionable. Laundering had been its original industry, but London society had discovered the benefits of the two kinds of spring water, purgative saline and sulphurous, and had declared both to be as excellent as that obtained at the already modish Tunbridge Wells. And so the little hamlet had become an elegant place of fine brick houses, terraces, courts, and passages, with leafy walks shaded by handsome elms and limes. There were many superior residences in the surrounding area, many of them set in spacious parks, but none of them could equal Greys, which was undoubtedly the most desirable property of them all.

They drove steadily up the main street, and then on toward the heath.

As the carriage was making its slow way out of Hampstead on its way to Greys, Philip was returning to Southvale House after his appointment. He'd been given a great deal of information and instruction concerning St. Petersburg, but his mind was on Rosalind as the carriage approached St. James's Place.

Before this day was out, the woman he loved more than anything else in the world would drive out of his life forever. All they had left were a few hours, stolen, forbidden hours that broke every rule of honor. He shouldn't have asked her to spend any time with him, but he hadn't been able to resist, he loved her too much.

He leaned his head back, gazing emptily at the seat opposite. Guilt ached through him, guilt that he'd ruined Rosalind's life, and guilt that he no longer loved or wanted a wife he felt in his heart had betrayed her vows. He almost wished he was more like Gerald, capable of doing the dishonorable thing from time to time, but he wasn't, and so would stand by marriage vows that had ceased to have any meaning. He'd never discovered Celia in any indiscretion, so how could he possibly deny her now? Damn his conscience, damn his honor, and damn his sense of duty.

The carriage swayed to a standstill in the courtyard, and he climbed quickly down, hurrying up the doors and flinging them open before Richardson had even crossed the entrance hall.

"Where is Miss Carberry, Richardson?" he asked without preamble, for he needed to be with her for every second from now on.

"Miss Carberry has gone to Greys, my lord."

Philip paused in astonishment. "I beg your pardon."

At that moment Katherine came hurrying down the staircase. "Oh, Philip, I've got so much to tell you."

"Before you do, I want to know why Rosalind has gone to Greys." Philip tossed his tricorn on the table.

Katherine faced him. "To find Celia's love letters and bring them back here," she said.

"Celia's what?"

"Love letters. That's what I want to tell you, Philip. Rosalind won't have to leave now, of that I'm quite sure." Katherine proceeded to tell him everything that had happened, leaving absolutely nothing out. "Then I remembered that the tree-house repairs are to begin today," she finished, "and that's why Rosalind has gone on her own with Annie. We thought it best if I stayed here with Great-aunt Eleanor, who really has been upset by everything that's happened."

Philip was very still, and for a long, long moment he didn't say anything, but then he looked urgently at his sister. "Is Annie quite sure about those letters?"

"Yes, quite sure."

"They prove beyond all doubt that Celia and this Dom Rodrigo were lovers?"

"Yes."

He closed his eyes for a moment, hardly daring to hope that something would come of this. But if work had already commenced on the tree house, the letters may already have been destroyed. "How long ago did they leave, Katherine?"

"Well over an hour now."

"Then I think they may be in time."

Richardson had been standing nearby all the time, and his face had become increasingly anxious. "Begging your pardon, my lord . . ."

"What is it, Richardson?"

"It concerns Miss Carberry, my lord."

Philip's blue eyes sharpened as he detected the man's unease. "What about her?"

"Just before she left for Greys, Mr. Beaufort called to see her. I didn't know he was here, for his curricle must have drawn into the courtyard just as the traveling carriage came to the door. I entered the hall a few moments before he left again, and he was talking to Miss Carberry. Their voices were raised, my lord, and I'm quite sure that he was issuing a threat of some kind to her."

"A threat?" Philip's tone became cold and urgent.

"Yes, my lord. I—I don't remember his exact words, but I'm sure it was something to the effect that he intended to have his revenge over something. He certainly said that in the end she'd wish she'd never come to London."

Katherine was indignant. "How dare he presume to say such a thing! He's been a snake and a toad, and has the audacity to—"

"Be quiet Katherine," ordered Philip, his attention still on the butler. "What's this leading to, Richardson?"

"Well, when Mr. Beaufort realized I was there, he became all agreeability and very civilly requested me to send word to his residence that he wouldn't be returning for some time as he was going to the prizefight at Crawley Down."

"And?"

"And Lady Eleanor sent a man to Greys early this morning, to bring her some of the apples from the orchard, and he rode back only a short while ago. He said he passed Mr. Beaufort on the Hampstead Road, driving toward Greys as if the hounds of hell were on his tail. Hampstead is in the opposite direction to Crawley Down, and Mr. Beaufort cannot possibly be there and see the prizefight."

Katherine's breath caught and her hands crept to her cheeks.

The butler looked at Philip. "Greys is very isolated, my lord, and there'll be hardly anyone around because you aren't in residence. If Miss Carberry is going down to the lake and the tree house and if Mr. Beaufort intends to be there, too . . ."

"Have my best saddle horse brought around immediately," Philip said quickly.

"My lord." Richardson almost ran away across the hall.

Katherine looked tearfully at Philip. "You don't think Gerald would really do anything to her, do you?"

"I don't intend to take any chances, but I tell you this, if he harms so much as a single hair on her head, I'll tear his throat out."

"Will—will it take you long to ride there?"

"It's uphill most of the way," he reminded her, "but I think I can be there in just over fifteen minutes."

"I couldn't bear it if anything happened to her. I like her so much, Philip."

"I know you do," he said softly, pulling her close for a moment and hugging her. "Wipe your eyes now, and when you're composed, go to Great-aunt Eleanor."

"Shall I tell her what's happened?"

"I . . ."

He said no more, for that lady's imperious tone echoed down from far above. "Tell me what, Katherine?"

They both turned to see their great-aunt descending in her mauve silk wrap, her hair pushed up beneath a large frilled bonnet.

Philip nodded at Katherine. "Tell her everything, for she'll get it out of you anyway now she's sniffed that something's going on."

"I heard that, sir," remarked the old lady crossly. "What, exactly, is going on?"

"Katherine will tell you, Great-aunt. I'm afraid I have to ride to Greys."

"In those clothes? Philip, you're dressed almost for court, not for riding!"

'It's a long story, and I truly don't have the time now," he replied, turning and snatching up his tricorn.

The old lady stared after him as he strode out.

He ran to mount the mettlesome bay horse that a groom

was just leading to the door, and a moment later he was
urging it away between the gates and out into St. James Place.

Gerald had already reached Greys, but hadn't gone into
the estate by way of the main entrance, for he had no wish
to be seen. Instead, he'd driven the long way around, halting
his curricle in a shady dell on the far side of the park, just
outside the boundary wall. A large, very old yew tree hung
over very conveniently, and he climbed easily into it,
dropping down inside the park.

He could see the house standing white on the hill above,
but he'd chosen a place that was down almost on a level with
the lake. He paused cautiously for a moment, because Philip's
gamekeepers could be at work nearby, but everything seemed
to be quiet, so he walked quickly and quietly toward the lake,
which was just visible through the curtain of trees.

With each step he felt more at ease, and more certain of
carrying out his plan. He intended to retrieve the indiscreet
letters his foolish sister had apparently left to be discovered
by her damned maid. It wouldn't do for Celia to forfeit her
marriage, especially not when that haughty American stood
to gain. Soon he'd teach Miss Rosalind Carberry a lesson
she'd never forget. Her fortune would have been just the
thing for his financial predicament, and her charms would
have been very welcome in his bed, but she'd spurned him,
and for that she had to pay. Maybe he couldn't lay his hands
upon her fortune now, but he could still enjoy the lady's
charms, and he'd get away with it. He grinned to himself,
for wasn't he at this very moment one of the huge crowd
on Crawley Down? How could he possibly be there, and here
at Greys, forcing his unwelcome attentions upon a willful
American creature who'd come to England to destroy his
sister's marriage? Anything Rosalind Carberry said against
him would be put down to petty female spite, nothing more.

He could see the lake clearly now, the water flashing in
the sunlight. He paused for a moment, glancing around. The
tree house was plain to see on the tiny island, and just beyond

the Chinese bridge there was a particularly dense clump of rhododendrons, the perfect place to conceal himself and await events.

Moving swiftly along the shore and past the bridge, he pushed his way into the rhododendrons. The long, shining, dark-green leaves brushed against his face, their touch cold, but within a few moments it was impossible to tell he was there.

As he settled back to wait, Rosalind's carriage turned slowly in through the gates on the hill above and drove slowly toward the house.

23

⚜

As the carriage made its way toward the house, Rosalind still dreaded that work might already have started on the tree house. Her hands clasped and unclasped in her lap, and she was screwed up to such a pitch of nerves that she was barely aware of the house of which she yet had some hope of becoming the mistress. Opposite her, Annie sat in an equally anxious state, for the thought of Celia's imminent return was quite dreadful.

The carriage drew to a standstill before the house, and Rosalind glanced up at the shuttered windows. The main doors opened and a woman came out. She was of medium height, with sandy hair that was now sprinkled with gray. She had a not unkindly face and wore a maroon wool gown with a high neck and long tight sleeves. A starched white mob cap rested on her head, and her apron was very white and crisp. There was a large bunch of keys dangling on a chain from her belt, denoting that she was the housekeeper, Mrs. Simmons.

She approached the carriage, a smile on her face, for she expected to greet Philip, or possibly Lady Eleanor or Katherine; her lips parted in surprise as the coachman jumped down and opened the door for Rosalind to alight.

Bobbing a swift curtsy, the woman glanced briefly at Annie, who climbed down unaided. "May I be of assistance, madam?" she asked Rosalind.

"Can you tell me if work has commenced on the tree house yet?" inquired Rosalind, the fingers of her left hand crossed secretly.

The woman was taken aback. "I beg your pardon, madam?"

"The tree house, has work on it started yet?"

"Why, no, madam, but I expect the men to arrive at any moment."

Rosalind exhaled with relief and gave Annie a hopeful smile. "Thank goodness, we're in time."

Mrs. Simmons was perplexed. "Begging your pardon, madam, but are you Miss Carberry?"

"You know about me?"

"Yes, madam. Lady Eleanor sent a footman here earlier for some of her favorite apples. He told me. Is there something you require from the tree house, madam? Maybe I can send a man down there for you?"

"No, that's quite all right, we'll go down ourselves."

"There's no need to put yourself to such effort, madam."

"We'll go ourselves," repeated Rosalind, turning to Annie. "Lead the way, Annie."

"Yes, madam."

As they walked away across the gravel and then down into the park, the housekeeper glanced at the coachman. "So that's her, is it?"

"As pretty a piece of muslin as I've ever seen," he replied appreciatively, watching Rosalind's ankles as the light breeze played with her hem.

"You can always be relied upon to keep matters at a low level, James Patterson," observed Mrs. Simmons tartly. "Well, at least I now know why his lordship was here all that time without wanting anyone to know. He certainly did have something to think about, didn't he? What's she like?"

"Miss Carberry? A regular lady from all accounts. She's been good to Annie, that's for sure. You recall that Annie's mother has been unwell for some time?"

"Yes."

"Well, she got much worse and needed an operation. Miss Carberry told Annie she'd pay for everything."

Mrs. Simmons drew a long breath. "Then she's a vast improvement on what we're going to have back again, eh?"

"Reckon so."

"Attend to your horses, Mr. Patterson, and then come to the kitchens. I'm sure you have time to take a dish of tea with me."

"I doubt it, for they wish to drive back to town as soon as they can."

"What is it that they want with the tree house?" she asked, shading her eyes against the sun to watch Rosalind and Annie moving down through the park.

"I haven't a clue, Mrs. Simmons. I thought no one had used that place for years now, and as to why an American lady who's about to go back home would want to rush like the devil to see it, I really couldn't even begin to guess."

The housekeeper sighed and nodded. "All these years I've worked for the gentry, and I still don't really understand them properly." Shaking her head, she turned and went back into the house.

The coachman looked down through the park for a moment longer and then climbed back onto his perch, picking up the reins and urging the tired horses into action to drive them to the stables at the rear of the house. It was always quite a haul up here to Greys, but at least there was always the prospect of a good downhill run all the way back.

With Mrs. Simmons gone back into the house and the carriage removed to the stables, there was no one left to see what did or didn't take place down by the lake.

Unaware of the danger lying in wait for her, Rosalind was thinking about the letters and the wonderful possibility that they might make it possible for her to be with Philip, after all. But did she really dare to hope anything? She remembered how Celia had been when they'd spoken earlier. Philip's wife was devious, clever, and quick-witted, with a ready answer for everything; such an adversary would not be easily routed, not even when there was apparently overwhelming evidence against her.

The tree fringing the lake were close now. Fallen leaves rustled beneath their feet as they followed a barely discernible path toward the water. The air was cooler in the shade, and the smell of autumn was suddenly stronger. A magpie was alarmed by their approach, flying noisily to the topmost branches of a tree. Long-tailed, with black-and-white plumage and a tinge of blue on its wings, it was exactly the same as the magpies she knew at home. She remembered that just such a bird had flown across her path when she'd ridden out with John to keep her very first assignation with Philip. Was this magpie an omen, a warning that soon she'd be going back to Washington, after all?

"There's the tree house, Miss Carberry," Annie said, pointing ahead.

Rosalind saw the island and the beautiful Chinese bridge spanning the brief distance from the shore. The broad, spiky green leaves of irises grew in profusion by the bridge, where in summer their yellow flowers made a brave show of color. Nearby there were rhododenrons, also just leaves now, but in summer they would be brilliant with mauve, crimson, and white. Some swans sailed on the water, their orange-and-black legs pumping visibly because the lake was so clear. A light breeze stirred through the trees, detaching more leaves from their places.

Gazing at the little tree house, Rosalind thought how delicate and beautiful it was. It reminded her of the summerhouse in the rose garden at home; she was aware that it was the second time she'd thought of home within the past few minutes.

They reached the bridge, and as Annie went on across, something made Rosalind pause. She glanced back, searching the trees, and the park beyond. She felt vaguely uneasy, as if someone was watching her. Her glance lingered for a moment on the rhododendrons, but the breeze ruffled through them, making the shining leaves whisper together.

"Is something wrong, Miss Carberry?" Annie had halted on the far side of the bridge.

"I don't know. I thought . . ."

"Madam?"

"I thought someone was there."

The maid glanced past her, looking around. "I can't see anyone, Miss Carberry."

"No, nor can I." Rosalind smiled a little ruefully and then hurried on over the bridge.

They halted at the foot of the narrow wooden staircase, and Annie remembered how rickety and unsafe the handrail had been when last she'd come here. She tested it again, and it wobbled alarmingly from side to side.

"I'll hold the rail steady, Miss Carberry, and you go up first."

"All right." Gathering her skirts, Rosalind went gingerly up the steps toward the little doorway at the top. As she tentatively turned the handle and went inside, she didn't glance back once.

Annie watched from below, so intent upon what Rosalind was doing that she knew nothing of Gerald's approach until he'd grabbed her from behind. Before she could cry out, he clamped his hand roughly over her mouth. Terrified, she tried to twist free and see who her attacker was at the same time, but he struck her several times on the side of her head and she went limp in his grasp.

He glanced quickly up the steps, but Rosalind was inside the tree house and knew nothing of what was going on below. He quickly dragged the unconscious maid around the tree trunk, leaving her where she couldn't be seen from above.

For the briefest of moments he paused to look warily around, but still there was no sign of anyone on the estate, so he slowly began to go up the steps toward his unknowing victim.

Rosalind was still oblivious to the peril that was almost upon her. As she entered the little building, she turned immediately to look above the door. The loose board was easy to see, and she reached up to pull it away. A glad cry escaped her as she saw the bundle of letters behind, still tied with the red ribbon. Seizing it, she went to the broken window, where the sunlight flooded in.

Her hands trembled a little as she slipped the topmost letter from beneath the ribbon. The writing seemed to leap out at her, for it was exactly the same as that on the letter from Lisbon. The first few lines were all she needed to read, for they proved beyond all shadow of doubt that Celia had taken Dom Rodrigo de Freire as her lover: "My dearest, most beloved Celia, Words cannot describe how empty I feel this morning after waking up alone in the bed where you and I shared nights of incomparable passion . . ."

She heard a step in the doorway and thought it was Annie. "They're just as you said, Annie, indisputable evidence that Lady Southvale was unfaithful with Dom Rodrigo . . ." Folding the letter again, she turned, and her smile died away, freezing on her lips as she saw Gerald standing there.

His glance swept coolly over her and then came to rest on her suddenly pale face. "Do go on, my dear, for I'm finding it quite fascinating."

Her fingers closed in fear over the letter she'd been reading, and instinctively she held the rest of the bundle against her breast. "Where's Annie? What have you done to her?" she whispered fearfully.

"I've merely made certain that she doesn't interrupt us," he murmured, looking at the bundle of letters. "Celia's, I presume?"

"They're nothing. I—I just found them . . ."

He shook his head reprovingly and tutted a little. "Don't

tell fiblings, Rosalind, for it's most unbecoming. Those letters belong to my sister, and I think she should have them back, don't you?''

Rosalind didn't reply. Her heart was thundering in her breast, and she was terrified. He had her trapped, and short of flinging herself out of the window, there was nothing she could do to escape.

"Give me the letters, Rosalind," he said softly, holding out his hand.

She cast desperately around, but there was nothing she could do to get away from him. The tree house's walls enclosed them both, and she could see by his eyes that he had more than the retrieval of the letters on his mind.

"Give me the letters, Rosalind," he said again, and there was an edge to his voice.

Keeping the one letter still tightly gripped in her hand, so that he couldn't see it, she turned suddenly, flinging the rest of the bundle out the open window. She heard it fall with a splash into the lake, then she faced him again, her chin raised defiantly. "Go and get them," she said, being careful to conceal the one in her hand.

His hazel eyes were suddenly bright with fury and his lips curled back savagely as he lunged toward her. She screamed, but the sound was jerked from her as he flung her forcefully back against the wall and then pressed against her. His body was hard, and he pinched her chin between his fingers, his lips only inches from hers, so that she could feel his breath on her face.

"You shouldn't have done that, Rosalind, for you've made me angrier than ever now. I'm not accustomed to being crossed, and you've gone out of your way to thwart me, haven't you?''

"Let me go! Please!''

"I intend to take my pleasure of you, sweetheart, and no one's going to believe it was me.''

Her eyes were huge with terror as she stared at him. Her

heart was pounding unbearably, and she felt ice-cold, as if she stood naked in the depths of winter snow.

His fingers tightened, his nails digging into her skin. "I've made sure it's known I've gone to the prizefight, so who's going to think you're telling the truth when you claim I was here? No one saw me arrive, I made sure of that, and I'll make equally sure that no one sees me leave. There won't be a soul who'll believe you, my dear, for I'll see to it that they all know how you switched your attentions to me when Philip spurned you, and how spiteful you became when I declined your advances. You'll be known as a malicious, vengeful woman, Rosalind, set upon paying me back for not wanting you."

"Please," she whispered. "Please, let me go."

"All in good time, my lovely, all in good time." His voice was soft, and he pinned her against the wall with his weight, his hands roaming knowing over her body.

The letter fell unnoticed from her hand, for she was too frightened now to hold it. Her heart was beating so much that she thought it would burst, and her whole being recoiled in revulsion from his touch. She tried desperately to wrench herself free, but he was by far too strong for her.

Her struggles seemed to excite him. His face was flushed and his breathing heavy. His hands became more urgent, moving all over her, sliding sensuously against every curve and pressing where no man had ever touched her before. She wanted to cry out, but her voice was silent. Tears were wet on her cheeks, and she felt helpless to do anything to save herself. She was completely at his mercy, his to do with as he pleased.

She tried to avert her face, but his fingers forced her to look at him again. He bent his head, kissing her on the lips as if he would devour her. There was no skill in him, just a brutish desire, and he used his superior strength to deny her any chance of pulling away. He wanted her, and was aroused to take her.

Silent sobs caught in her throat as she felt him pulling at her skirts, dragging them up to reveal her legs. His hand touched her naked thigh, his fingers pinching to hold her tightly.

An agonized fear engulfed her. She already felt violated, stained forever by his lust, and it was going to be much, much worse than this. There was no loving tenderness, no caressing, no gentleness, just animal force, savage and wild.

She closed her eyes, as if to shut everything out, and she tried to whisper Philip's name. Philip, I love you. I love you . . .

He ripped at the buttons of her pelisse and then at the throat of the gown beneath, but then, quite suddenly, he gave a grunt and his hold relaxed. He released her, whirling about, and then his head jerked back sickeningly as someone's fist caught him violently on the jaw.

Rosalind was frozen, unable to move as she watched him slump to the floor. She stared at him, her thoughts so scattered and frightened that she didn't know what had happened.

"Rosalind?" Someone was touching her again, trying to hold her close.

"No," she screamed and battered her fists against him. "No, leave me alone! Don't touch me!"

"Rosalind, it's me, Philip."

The helplessly beating fists became still and her breath caught. "Philip?" She looked at him then, and tears of unutterable relief stung her eyes. "Oh, Philip . . ."

He crushed her close, his hand holding her head tightly against his shoulder. "Are you all right?" he whispered. "Did he . . . ?"

"I'm all right," she said softly, her voice barely audible because of the bewildering emotions spinning wildly through her. She was safe, she was safe . . .

For a long moment they stood there, and then he gently drew back. "Are you really all right?"

"Just shaken, that's all. Oh, Philip, if you hadn't come

when you did . . .'' She looked at him, searching his face. ''But why have you come?''

''It's a long story; I'll explain later. For the moment, however, we have to make sure of Gerald.'' He glanced at her jockey bonnet and the long gauze scarf trailing from it. ''We'll tie him with your scarf.''

She nodded, turning slightly for him to untie the scarf, then she watched as he knelt by Gerald, who was just beginning to stir. Philip rolled him roughly over onto his stomach, almost wrenching his arms behind his back and tying his wrists tightly with the scarf, wrapping and knotting it so many times that it couldn't possibly be worked free, no matter how diligently Gerald may twist his hands.

Gerald's eyes flickered and opened.

Philip immediately pressed his face to the damp floor. ''You'll pay dearly for what you've done, Beaufort.''

''I'll deny everything.''

''Deny it if you wish, it makes no odds, for I intend to have your heart out for this. I curse the day I ever heard the name Beaufort.''

Gerald's mouth was distorted against the floor, but he still maanged a mocking grin. ''You have a Beaufort wife, de Grey, and nothing's going to change that. There aren't any letters now, because your paramour threw them into the lake. Now you'll never prove anything against Celia.''

Rosalind bent to pick up the letter she'd detached from the bundle, and she showed it to Philip. ''I did't throw them all away, Philip, and this one says all you need to know.''

Getting up from the floor, he read the letter, then he smiled at her. ''Not even Celia can deny this.'' He held out his hand to her, drawing her close.

Her lips trembled as she raised her face to his, and she closed her eyes as he kissed her.

Then he pulled away, putting the letter in his pocket and taking out a large, freshly laundered handkerchief, which he proceeded to unfold and roll into a makeshift rope to tie around Gerald's ankles.

"That should keep him still for the time being," he said, straightening again. "I'll send some men down to collect him in a short while."

Gerald tried to twist his head to look at him. "What are you going to do with me, de Grey?"

"The law can deal with you. Assault is a serious charge."

"I'll see to it that her name is dragged through every morsel of mud I can find, just remember that."

Philip didn't say anything, but took Rosalind's hand again, leading her to the door and down the steps to the grass below.

Annie was sitting up and leaning dazedly against the tree trunk, for not only had Gerald struck her, but she'd hit her head when she'd fallen. She was aware of where she was, but was momentarily confused as to why she was there. Then memory returned, and with a gasp she tried to get up, but Rosalind put a gentle hand on her shoulder. "It's all right, Annie, it's all over now."

"The letters—"

"They were there, just as you said," interrupted Rosalind reassuringly, glancing across the bridge to where Philip's foam-flecked, sweating horse was standing.

Annie looked anxiously at her. "Will you be staying with us, Miss Carberry?"

Rosalind smiled. "Yes, Annie, I will."

The maid closed her eyes with relief, but then looked puzzled. "I was watching you climb the steps to the tree house, and then—"

"I think Mr. Beaufort struck you."

Annie stared at her. "Mr. Beaufort?"

"He's still up there, his lordship knocked him down and tied him securely. Do you think you can stand, Annie?"

"I—I think so."

Rosalind and Philip helped her to get up; she swayed for a moment, feeling a little weak and giddy, but then she smiled again. "I'm all right, truly I am, I . . . ." Her voice broke off in horror as she saw Rosaslind's torn clothes.

"It was Mr. Beaufort, but I'm quite all right. I'll tell you about it later," said Rosalind quickly, not feeling ready to talk about it just yet, it was all too painful and fresh.

Philip looked at the maid. "We'll get you across the bridge and put you on my horse to go up to the house."

"Thank you, my lord. My lord . . . ?"

"Yes?"

"I shouldn't be here, her ladyship dismissed me." Annie's conscience weighed heavily.

"I know, I've been told all about it this morning." He smiled a little. "Your position here is secure, so have no fear on that score."

Tears came to Annie's eyes. "Thank you, my lord."

He lifted the injured maid into his arms and carried her across the bridge, putting her gently on the horse. "Hold on tightly, now," he instructed, "for it wouldn't do for you to fall and hurt yourself again, would it?"

"No, my lord."

He turned to Rosalind, his blue eyes tender, then he held out his hand to her. "I'll confront Celia with the letter tonight," he said softly. His fingers closed warmly and lovingly around hers, and they began to walk away from the lake.

24

Constables were sent for to deal with Gerald, who tried to claim that he was there to keep an assignation with Rosalind, but the constables made it plain they didn't believe him. They'd come up against Mr. Gerald Beaufort in the past and knew him for a slippery, untrustworthy, unscrupulous blackguard, one whom they were only too delighted to take into custody.

One of the constables happened to be Mrs. Simmons' cousin, and he lent a very sympathetic ear to her request that Rosalind's name was to be protected at all costs. The housekeeper had as little desire as everyone else to see Celia given any advantage, including the possibility of Philip's new love being falsely shamed in court. The constable lost no time in privately warning Gerald to drop all mention of Miss Carberry's so-called participation in a liaison with him, otherwise there would be other charges brought against him, the nature of which the constable hadn't yet decided, but they ranged from demanding money with menaces to horse-stealing.

Knowing that the man would carry out his threat and would concoct a variety of imaginary charges, Gerald wisely decided to omit Rosalind's name from everything from then on. Philip preferred to protect her as much as possible, and so it was decided to charge Gerald with the assault upon Annie, and not with the attempted rape in the tree house. It meant a less severe sentence, but at least Rosalind's name and reputation wouldn't be called into question in court.

When Gerald had been removed from the estate and into custody, Philip, Rosalind, and Annie drove back to London with the letter, with which it was intended to face Celia when she came to Southvale House at seven o'clock that evening.

It was late afternoon when the carriage turned in through the gates from St. James's Place, and Richardson hurried out immediately, a glad smile breaking out on his face when Philip quickly told him that all was well. Katherine ran down the stairs to meet them in the entrance hall, and although appalled and outraged to hear of the depths to which Gerald had sunk, she was overjoyed to see the single surviving letter.

Lady Eleanor was pleased, too, but couldn't allow herself to be too certain that the letter was definite proof until Philip's lawyer, Sir Henry Baillie-Drummond, had examined it. An urgent message was sent to Sir Henry's residence in Conduit Street, and he came immediately. He declared that the letter would indeed satisfy any court that Lady Southvale had betrayed her marriage vows, and that the other letter, from Portugal, would satisfy that same court that the infidelity had continued for well over a year. He pronounced that under such circumstances, Philip was certain to be granted his freedom.

Seven o'clock was approaching, and Philip prepared to face his wife in the library. Rosalind, Lady Eleanor, and Katherine gathered silently in the adjoining room, which was separated by tall folding doors through which the conversation could be clearly overheard.

Rosalind had taken great care with her appearance and wore the gray velvet evening gown. Celia wasn't likely to arrive looking anything less than her glorious best, and even now Rosalind was conscious of how powerfully beautiful and fascinating her adversary was. Celia was bound to do her best to deny the letter, or to explain it away, and there was still the ghost of a chance that she could stir Philip's heart to memories of the past. Rosalind knew that he no longer loved Celia, but she also knew it would be a foolish woman indeed who underestimated a foe as clever and enterprising as Celia Beaufort.

The clocks were just beginning to strike the hour when a carriage drove into the courtyard. Philip heard it and went to take up his position by the library fire, standing with his back toward it, his hands clasped behind him. He wore a purple corded-silk coat with black velvet lapels, and white silk breeches. A diamond pin flashed in his neckcloth, catching the mixture of firelight and candlelight, and his coal-black hair was a little tousled, for he'd run his fingers through it a moment before. He didn't relish the thought of the forthcoming interview, for he'd loved Celia very much in the past, but given her present intention to return to him under the cover of a barrage of lies—and to return at Rosalind's expense—he knew that she had to be faced with the truth and that he was the one who had to do it.

In the adjoining room, where only firelight illuminated the darkness, the three women waited with bated breath. Lady Eleanor couldn't bear it and sat by the fire, out of earshot, but both Katherine and Rosalind stood by the folding doors, Katherine with her ear pressed to the wood, Rosalind managing to peep through the tinest crack. She couldn't see a great deal, just the corner of a great writing desk and the velvet curtains at one of the windows.

They all heard the main doors of the house open and close and the murmur of voices as Richardson admitted Celia. The butler had been well-primed as to what to say, and he gave no sign that anything was amiss as he conducted his old mistress up to the library.

He tapped on the door and then opened it, announcing her. "Lady Southvale, my lord."

Celia's skirts rustled richly as she entered, and she halted right where Rosalind could see her. She looked as breathtakingly beautiful as Rosalind had suspected, her dark hair dressed up in shining curls through which strings of tiny pearls had been looped. There were more strings of pearls around her throat and resting against the curve of her creamy bosom. Her gown was made of oyster taffeta, with a very low and daring square neckline and little puffed sleeves. She wore long pale-pink gloves, and there was a lacy shawl of the same pink draped over her slender arms.

Her lilac eyes shone and her lips were soft as she smiled at Philip. "I didn't think I was ever going to see you again, my darling," she whispered, and to Rosalind's amazement and reluctant admiration, she managed to squeeze some tears so that they shimmered adorably on her long lashes. Her lips trembled with emotion, and she gave every appearance of being overcome with emotion just at seeing him again.

It was an acting *tour de force*; in the past it would have exerted its intended spell over Philip, but tonight it didn't touch him. "You're looking as beautiful as ever, Celia," he observed, almost conversationally.

"Is that all you have to say?"

"No, Celia, I have a great deal to say."

She hurried to him, out of Rosalind's sight.

Philip caught Celia's hands as she reached up, meaning to link her arms around his neck. "No, Celia, for I do not intend to take you back."

She drew slowly away, her lilac eyes suddenly guarded. "What do you mean?"

"I mean exactly what I say."

"But I'm your wife, Philip."

"A fact that you seem to have conveniently forgotten for some time now."

Celia turned away, her fingertips dragging lightly across the corner of the writing desk, then she turned to face him again, standing where Rosalind could see her. "I suppose I can guess whose hand is behind this," she said, managing to put a sad little tremble in her voice. "You must know by now that I met your Miss Carberry this morning. She made it plain that she would stop at nothing to get her scheming hands on you, and this is obviously the result. I nearly died in that shipwreck, Philip, and would have died if that Portuguese ship hadn't passed by. I've been very ill, and very frightened. Have you any idea what it's like to have lost one's memory? I didn't know who I was, where I came from, or anything . . .'' She turned away, her voice catching on a very convincing sob.

"You missed your vocation, Celia," he said, "for you should have gone on the stage."

"How can you say that," she cried, swaying a little to signify that she was almost overwhelmed with hurt and disbelief.

"Oh, stop all this, Celia, for we both know it's an act," he snapped, placing the two letters on the writing desk before her. "Look at these, and then let's see what you have to say."

She turned quickly, her eyes flying to the accusing sheets of paper. The sobs halted on a gasp and a little of the color drained from her face, but she recovered quickly. "I have no idea what they are," she said, so admirably feigning bewildered innocence that even Rosalind could have believed her.

Philip picked the love letter up and began to read: "My dearest, most beloved Celia, Words cannot describe how empty I feel this morning after waking up alone in the bed where you and I shared nights of incomparable passion . . ." He looked at his wife. "Shall I go on?"

"If you wish to read out the scribbles of an infatuated admirer of mine, then please do."

"Dom Rodrigo was an infatuated admirer, was he?"

"Yes. He was very persistent and became troublesome, but in the end he accepted that I didn't wish to have anything to do with him. I was never unfaithful to you, my darling."

"Weren't you?"

Immeasurable hurt shone reproachfully in Celia's magnificent eyes, fresh tears shimmered on her lashes, and her lips trembled appealingly. "Oh, Philip," she whispered, "How could you doubt me?"

"Perhaps because both these letters are in Dom Rodrigo's hand. Evidently your shared nights of incomparable passion soon became eminently forgettable as far as she was concerned, for in this other letter he'd have me believe he didn't even know who you were. Quite astonishing, don't you think?"

She couldn't think of anything to say.

"Aren't you going to deny it all, Celia?" he inquired.

"It would seem a little pointless."

"Yes, it would indeed. How very foolish of you to leave those letters behind."

"How were they discovered?"

"Because I chose to redecorate Greys, and because the maid you'd so heartlessly and casually dismissed found them. She meant to use them to force a reference out of you."

"Annie is responsible for this?" she whispered venomously.

"No, Celia, you are responsible. Oh, I'd long suspected you of adultery, but you were too clever to be caught, and in the absence of any proof, I felt I had no option but to accept that you were, after all, a faithful and loving wife. Even after I fell in love with Rosalind, I was prepared to give her up because I felt I had a duty toward you, but in the end you've been the architect of your own downfall, Celia. If you hadn't been so disagreeable in the past, if you hadn't been so selfishly determined to have your own way at no matter what cost to anyone else, you'd have succeeded in worming your way back here. But you treated Annie with contempt, and so she kept the letters when she found them. You pulled the rug out from under your own feet, and if you've fallen flat because of it, you have no one to blame but yourself."

"I'm still your wife."

"Not for much longer. I've already instructed Sir Henry Baillie-Drummond that I wish to end our marriage."

She stared at him. "I don't believe you, you can't be doing this!"

"I am doing it, Celia, and as soon as I can, I intend to marry Rosalind."

"Gerald will call you out!"

Philip gave a short laugh. "He'll have to do so from behind bars, I fear."

Her eyes widened. "What do you mean?"

"He's in custody, Celia, for assaulting Annie." He made no mention of the attack on Rosalind.

Celia exhaled slowly, placing her hands on the writing desk and bowing her head for a moment. "So he didn't go to the prize-fight," she said quietly. Then she looked at him. "I'm not one to fight against insuperable odds, Philip. Set me aside if you wish, for I cannot deny the letters."

"I intend to, and I would be grateful if you'd leave this house right now."

The lovely eyes swept brightly over him. "I made a very foolish mistake when I allowed myself to become infatuated with Rodrigo, for I can see now, when it's too late, what I turned my back on."

"Just go, Celia," he said quietly.

Without another word, she turned and walked from the room.

Katherine hurried away from the folding doors, peeping secretly out onto the landing as Celia passed toward the staircase. Rosalind opened the folding doors and went to Philip.

He still stood by the desk, and he turned the moment he heard her. He caught her hand, pulling her quickly into his arms, and held her tight. "It's over now, my darling," he whispered, his voice muffled against her hair. "I love you so much, dear God, how I love you!"

"And I love you," she whispered back, savoring his closeness.

"I don't know when I'll be free, but I promise you that I'll make you the second Lady Southvale the moment I can."

"I know."

"When I think how close we came to parting forever—"

"But we didn't," she interrupted softly, "and now we'll always be together." She lifted her lips to meet his.

About six weeks later, on a dark Christmas Eve night, the air was so cold that stray flakes of snow fluttered down over London. Holly, mistletoe, and ivy decorated doors and windows, and the sound of carols could be heard in the streets. Stagecoaches were laden with passengers and luggage as people returned to their families for the festive season, and thoughts of war, either with America or with France, were temporarily set aside. The war with France was still very much in evidence, however, and a war with America was still very much in the cards, for Philip's errand from Washington had as yet come to nothing.

But at Southvale House the atmosphere couldn't have been more happy, even though Philip would soon be departing for St. Peterburg. Gerald was still behind bars—and would be for quite a while yet, because the judge took a very poor view of a gentleman assaulting a poor maid. Celia had tactfully removed herself to her astonished family in Ireland, who had to contend not only with her apparent return from the dead, but also with the scandal of a divorce, proceedings for which were now well under way.

London society had been equally as astonished to learn what had been happening in Lord Southvale's household, but few spared a great deal of sympathy for Celia, whose conduct was deemed to be odious in the extreme. Rosalind was made welcome wherever she went, and everyone wanted to hear the story in detail. It was thought to be romantic and almost gothic for Philip, the grieving widower, to have fallen in love with a beautiful American, only to have his vindictive, malicious, and spiteful wife return to resume her claim to him.

Annie was now one of the happiest maids in England, for she was to attend Rosalind permanently. Word had arrived from Falmouth that Hetty was now completely well again, and on the point of marrying Samuel Penruthin, which meant that she could no longer attend to her duties with Rosalind. All was well that ended well for both maids, and Rosalind wasn't at all displeased, for she'd been dreading the thought of having to discard Annie's services when Hetty returned.

There was so very much to tell everyone back in Washington that a very lengthy letter indeed had had to be written, explaining absolutely everything and begging them to come to London in the summer, when Philip hoped to have returned from St. Petersburg, and the wedding could at long last take place.

Rosalind was very happy that Christmas Eve and had never felt more lighthearted and carefree as she went down the staircase to the drawing room. She wore a cherry-red velvet gown, with matching ribbons in her golden hair. Diamonds sparkled at her throat and in her ears, and her green eyes shone.

Garlands of greenery were festooned everywhere, looped with crimson and gold ribbons, and the scent of clove oranges drifted from the huge ball that had been suspended from the entrance hall roof.

Philip seemed to sense that she was there, and he came out on to the landing.

She paused, a hand on the balustrade. Her fingertips brushed against leaves of mistletoe and ivy, and she smiled at him. "This is the most wonderful Christmas of my life," she whispered.

"And of mine," he replied, coming to take her in his arms.

They lingered over the kiss, lost in each other and totally unaware of Richardson hastening to the main doors as a travel-stained carriage came to a standstill in the courtyard.

A rather curt American voice addressed the astonished butler. "Is this Lord Southvale's residence?"

"Er, yes, sir. Who shall I say has called?"

"Mr. John Carberry."

Rosalind heard her brother's voice and turned incredulously to look down.

John came in, tossing his top hat on to the silver-topped

table. Then he removed his cloak and dropped that there too. Underneath he wore a blue coat and fawn breeches, and he looked as if he'd been traveling for some time without any halts. His green eyes, so like Rosalind's own, looked tired, and his golden hair was disheveled, but not intentionally so.

He turned to face the startled butler. "Is Miss Carberry here?"

Rosalind began to hurry gladly down to him, the cherry ribbons in her hair fluttering. "Yes, John, I'm here. Oh, I'm so happy to see you!" She flung herself into her brother's arm, almost in tears of joy at having him arrive so unexpectedly.

He held her for a moment and then drew back, his eyes serious. "Are you all right?"

"All right? Oh, yes!" She smiled at him.

His gaze moved beyond her, to Philip, who was just coming down to join them. "What's been going on here, Southvale?" he demanded coldly.

Southvale? Rosalind was dismayed, her smile fading. "John? What is it?"

John's green eyes were level and uncompromising as they rested on Philip. "You sent a very brief and very insulting note to my sister, sir, and I'm here to see what's damned well going on!"

Rosalind stared at her brother. "John?"

He took her hand. "A note arrived from London for you after you'd left, and under the circumstances we felt it best to read it. It rather abruptly instructed you not to come to London. Father and I decided that I should come here to see that you were all right."

"Well, I am all right, as you can see, so . . ."

John looked at Philip again. "Why did you write it, Southvale?"

Philip held his gaze. "I admit that it was woefully inadequate, and I deeply regret it now, but something had happened that made it vital that I prevented Rosalind from leaving."

"Indeed? Well, it so happens that it might never have arrived at all, for the packet it came on, the *Queen of Falmouth*, was feared lost in storms."

Rosalind lowered her eyes gladly. So the *Queen of Falmouth* hadn't been lost after all.

Philip looked at her brother. "John . . ."

"I would prefer you not to address me by that name for the time being, sir, not until you've explained everything, and I'm satisfied that you've treated my sister honorably."

"Then I suggest you join us all in the drawing room, Mr. Carberry," Philip replied levelly. "It's a very long and complicated story, but I think you will be John to me again once you've heard it all."

Rosalind linked her brother's arm. "He's right, John, you will. He hasn't behaved poorly toward me—in fact, quite the opposite. You must believe me."

John hesitated, knowing that she meant every word. "I want to believe you, Rosalind, for I want you to be happy. You know that, don't you? All I'm concerned with is your welfare, because you're my sister and I love you."

At that moment Katherine appeared by the balustrade above, looking very sweet and pretty in a lemon organdy muslin gown. She looked curiously down. "What's going on? Great-aunt Eleanor and I are growing tired of waiting for you two to join us . . ." Her voice died away as she saw John. "Oh, I do beg your pardon. I didn't realize someone had called."

John stared up at her, and she smiled at him.

Rosalind glanced speculatively at her brother. "John, there's someone I want you to meet, someone I'm sure you will like very much indeed. May I introduce Miss de Grey, Philip's sister?"

John still stared at Katherine. "Miss de Grey," he murmured.

Rosalind turned to Katherine. "This is my brother, John, Katherine."

Katherine came down the staircase toward them, smiling

at him again. "I'm so very pleased to meet you, Mr. Carberry. Rosalind has told me so much about you."

A little color had entered John's cheeks as he bowed over her hand, and there was a new softness in his eyes as he smiled at her. "I trust that I shall soon learn all about you too, Miss de Grey," he said.

"Do come up and meet Great-aunt Eleanor. Will you be staying for Christmas? Oh, please say you will . . ." Katherine took the arm he offered, and together they proceeded up the staircase.

In the entrance hall, Philip went to put his hand to Rosalind's chin, raising it so that he could look sternly into her eyes. "Are you hoping to make a match for my sister, madam?"

"I most certainly am, sir."

"Fie on you."

"And on you, sir," she replied coquettishly.

He laughed, pulling her into his arms and kissing her.

SIGNET REGENCY ROMANCE
COMING IN APRIL 1990

Marjorie Farrell
MISS WARE'S REFUSAL

Emily Hendrickson
THE COLONIAL UPSTART

Emma Lange
THE SCOTTISH REBEL